PRAISE FOR PETER DANISH'S "THE TENOR"

"Mr. Danish's writing is art in itself."

— *The Book Corner*

"Peter Danish's novel is an incredible and beautiful story."

— *Princess Eboli Reviews*

"Mr. Danish offers the reader an experience that only few authors are capable of generating."

— *L'Idea Magazine*

"Peter Danish's novel "The Tenor" is beyond remarkable!"

— *Jorie Loves a Story.com*

"A book of superb storytelling. Danish's sentences are silky and lush with musicality of prose and mesmerizingly lyrical writing."

— *The Hook of a Book Blog*

"There is no repose or standstill in Peter Danish's smooth and untiring prose!"

— *Book Reviews Unlimited*

"Peter Danish's story telling ability is lyrical and powerful"

— *Victoria Livengood, Metropolitan Opera*

"Mr. Danish's words fly off the page!"

— *BroadwayWorld.com*

D0841880

MEDJUGORJE
МЕДЈУГОРЈE

THE FINAL PROPHECY

By
Peter Danish

TRUE
N★RTH
PUBLISHING

Published by True North Publishing
Imprint of Motivational Press
1777 Aurora Road
Melbourne, Florida, 32935
www.MotivationalPress.com

Manufactured in the United States of America.

ISBN: 978-1-62865-230-7

Table of contents

PROLOGUE
ПРОЛОГУЕ

Medjugorje: A place of miracles

In 1981, two young girls in the former Yugoslavia reported seeing the Blessed Virgin Mary on a hilltop in a small town in southern Herzegovina. She called herself "Gospa." Since that day, millions of people have made the pilgrimage to the site. Hundreds have reported miraculous cures. The Catholic Church has yet to render judgment on the visions or the cures and medical science is at a loss to explain them. Pilgrims of all races, creeds, and colors continue to visit the shrine, each in hope of a miracle.

All accounts, photos, letters, oral testimonies, medical certificates, attest to miraculous healings in Medjugorje, and it is making some Catholic officials very uncomfortable. The Marxist Yugoslav state discouraged visits to Medjugorje, but the phenomenon could not be contained and interest has grown worldwide.

Studies were conducted by medical teams from several universities and the results of these analyses were negative. The doctors found no evidence of any kind of hoax. The boys and girls were not ill. They were not lying. They were of average intelligence and came from normal farming families, "no better or worse than others their age." They showed no signs of any psychological disorders.

Unfortunately, the same tranquility and good spirits exhibited by the Medjugorje visionaries have not characterized critics of the phenomenon. Even Catholics disagree on the authenticity of the experience. Despite everything, more confessions are heard each year in Medjugorje than in any other parish in the entire world; more than one hundred confessors work without interruption every day. And every year that number grows. Clearly, something is going on in Medjugorje.

"It is in vain that we pretend to arrive at the fullness of truth by reasoning. By this way we reach only rational truth."

"All mystics speak the same language, for they come from the same country."

- Louis Claude de St. Martin

Our Lady's message given through Mirjana, June 24, 1981.

Dear Children! I am calling you because I need you.
I need hearts ready for immeasurable love –
hearts that are not burdened by frivolity –
hearts that are ready to love as my Son loved –
hearts that are ready to sacrifice themselves as my Son sacrificed Himself.
I need you. In order to come with me, forgive yourselves, forgive others and adore my Son.
Adore Him also for those who have not come to know Him, for those who do not love Him.
Therefore, I need you; therefore, I call you.

CHAPTER 1

THE BUS

Herzegovina-Neretva Canton
Bosnia and Herzegovina
September 2012
Thursday, 2:15pm

After driving for over an hour on a bus that stank of stale cigarettes and which had no bathroom, if one excluded the plastic bucket behind the driver's seat, Tony Marshall's bladder was crying for relief. Some people who have quit smoking are so repulsed by the smell of cigarettes that they can get physically ill. Luckily he wasn't one of them, because the vast majority of the men, women, and children he'd met so far in Bosnia all smelled of cigarettes. He'd been a smoker himself earlier in life, but he never left the house without mints or breath spray. Years of smoking had shortened his breath noticeably and today he was really feeling it.

The day before, he'd played soccer with some kids he'd met in Mostar, probably the first time he'd done so in twenty years. Consequently, his entire body was full of tiny aches and pains. He moved about on the leatherette seat but couldn't manage to find a comfortable position. He leaned his head against the window and felt what passed for air-conditioning, a warm musty breeze poured forth from the tiny vent. The smell was difficult to describe, it was rank and pungent and Tony shuddered to think of just what particulate matter he might be inhaling.

He was grateful for the leatherette seats—the cloth ones on the bus to Mostar nearly made him sick. Oddly, they didn't seem to bother any of the other passengers in the slightest. He guessed the decades of cigarette smoke exposure must have completely corrupted their senses of smell.

He pressed his cheek against the window and glanced out at a slate gray sky and ominous clouds, rain was imminent—again. He knew the Bosnian word for rooms was *sobe*, so when they passed the hand-painted sign by the side of the road reading "*Sobe - 5 km*," he knew relief was in sight. The past two hours had been among the most challenging of the entire trip. This bunch was harder to get through to than any of the others, and that included those paranoid old ladies in Tuzla who looked at him like he was some kind of serial killer. But most cases, the greater the effort, the greater the reward. And this group of "pilgrims," as he called them—since they were all headed to a holy shrine—was absolutely priceless in both its ethnic and its religious make-up; it was like a microcosm of the entire former Yugoslavia on one bus. That is, of course, assuming that his assumptions regarding their nationalities were correct. The rest stop ahead would be an ideal spot to test his hypothesis about them. It would also provide a welcome breath of fresh air, some hot coffee and, presumably, a working 21st century bathroom.

It had been pouring rain on and off for the entire ride between Mostar and Medjugorje and the twisting and turning, narrow mountain roads made him nervous. The driver and his assistant seemed to know every bend and bump like the back of their hands, although exactly why the driver needed an assistant remained a mystery to Tony. The tourist guide in Mostar had listed the trip as being only forty five minutes long, but they were running closer to two hours and still weren't even close.

Despite the rain, it was oppressively hot and humid. The trees along the way were dull and lifeless, with tired-looking branches drooping as if from exhaustion. Every village they'd passed appeared asleep or in hibernation. No one stirred in the streets or in the scattered cottages that dotted the hillside.

Southern Bosnia and Herzegovina (the Herzegovina part) didn't have much physical appeal to him. Certainly nothing compared to the spectacular vistas of Sarajevo and the magnificent gorges and valleys of the Neretva and the Una Rivers. After they'd passed the last village, the foliage slowly gave way to lonely, treeless hills whose only dwellers were the occasional handful of meandering sheep. It looked like something out of the southwestern United States to him; not quite barren, but frontier-like wilderness.

Before long, they started to ascend one of the myriad mountain roads and the landscape radically, almost miraculously, changed to evergreens and dense foliage.

"Savagely beautiful," was how the tour guide had described this part of the country, and Tony agreed. He even felt the term extended accurately to most of the people he'd met here as well. These were folks who had been raised under the cloud of Communism and were permanently scarred by the worst war since WWII and the worst atrocities since the Holocaust. It was readily apparent in even their mundane daily routine. Tony noticed that even the simplest supermarket purchase was a major decision. Coming from a life of pointless excess, at first he found their thrift refreshing, but soon it saddened him to think that every expense had to be weighed in terms of whether or not it was necessary for basic survival.

It was more than just their thrift; given their history, that was understandable. He wasn't sure if it was a Slavic thing or a Balkan thing or a war-survivor thing, but these folks were different from any other people he'd ever met before. They were as a whole quiet, distant and unemotional; but there was something else, something strangely disquieting about them and something cabalistic about this whole country. Yet, he had to admit to himself, it was this very quality that had drawn him to this place and these people. Perhaps it said more about him than them.

He found it quite telling that, culturally, the most studied artwork of the region were in fact the gravestones. They were also the principal instrument of historical research in the region and they could be found hanging or displayed in both galleries and museums. The earliest written records of the region were compiled by Franciscan Monks, and they could always be relied upon to provide a nicely slanted view of the history of the area.

He had absolutely no reason to support it, but a heavy, dark sensation filled him and never quite allowed him to completely let his guard down and relax. In the cities, the old Stalin-era architecture, which provided an interesting historical curiosity in the light of day, was positively spectral at night, thoroughly imbuing the countryside with a sense of menace. As if it needed more of that! Seen through a filmmaker's eyes, this part of the world was a location scout's dream come true. That is to say, excepting the land mines, of course.

As a child, his grandmother had told him stories about Eastern Europe during WWII, saying that lands where so much blood had been spilt gave off an aura, a palpable sensation of its own. He now understood precisely what she'd meant. Make no mistake though— these folks were made from strong stuff. First they managed to successfully fight off Hitler during World War II and then, for half a century, Tito had kept his Yugoslavia the most independent of all the Communist block countries. That said something. Tito himself was a real piece of work and a damn cheeky bastard. Tony marveled at how Tito famously told Joseph Stalin to back off in a letter:

From Tito to Stalin—

"Please stop sending people to kill me. We've already captured five of them. If you don't stop sending assassins, I'll send one to Moscow, and I promise you I won't have to send a second."

—Josip Broz Tito

Ironically, for a place with such a violent history, faith ran especially fervent in this secluded part of Europe. Thus, it came as no great surprise when he heard that little children in this country were seeing visions of the Virgin Mary. Not only this, but the visions were also being accompanied by cryptic almost apocalyptic messages. Although he considered himself a spiritual person, he no longer followed any organized religion. He always felt that it was better to possess a mind that was open with curiosity than one closed off by religion. If he'd heard a report of mystic visions coming from somewhere in California, or someplace else in the U.S., he'd have just shaken his head and dismissed it with an incredulous laugh. But the fact that they were said to be happening *here* made him sit up and take notice. For reasons he could not explain, in this land, the strange and bizarre seemed commonplace. The impossible seemed possible.

He remembered the first time he'd ever heard the name Medjugorje. He was sitting outside a tiny coffee shop in Santa Monica, waiting for Claire to meet him after attending church. She'd heard the story of the little visionaries from the parish priest during his homily, going as far as to ask the congregation to pray for them.

As she retold the tale, Tony sensed immediately that this one would stick with him. A topic for a screenplay probably. People, especially young people, loved that supernatural crap, he thought. After doing a little homework of his own, he was hooked. No story he'd heard in ages had simultaneously aroused his curiosity and inquisitiveness while completely eluding any explanation he could come up with. He loved mysteries but he hated being baffled, and that was where he sat; clueless.

Why couldn't he simply dismiss it as a hoax or mass hallucination or the fantasy of a self-deluding, superstitious people? Four years later, he was still no closer to an answer. But he hoped, even prayed, that that would all change in the next twenty four hours. At the border crossing, from Croatia into Bosnia, the border police had come aboard the bus to check everyone's papers. As usual they were brandishing more medals and ribbons on their chest than a four-star general, and of course at least one of them carried the perfunctory submachine gun designed to put terror into the hearts of the less suspecting.

Tony vividly remembered the first time he saw the soldiers board a bus with their weapons drawn. His heart raced like a hummingbird and he perspired almost to the point of dehydration. Looking at his sweating and shaking, the soldiers first thought he might be dangerous, but upon closer inspection they realized he was just a wimp who had never seen a weapon before, let alone had one pointed at him.

Accordingly, they immediately seized the opportunity to fuck with him, driving him nearly to the point of tears with their questions and suspicious looks. Once they were convinced he'd need a change of underwear, they left. Tony immediately went to work on a mental list of things not to do when someone is holding a submachine gun to your face.

He opened his backpack and pulled out a notebook. The backpack was all the luggage he carried. Not by design, but through the courtesy and hard work of Air Croatia, who had managed to lose his rolling suitcase when he landed back in Split.

Standing at the baggage carousel, which was rapidly thinning out, Tony had that sinking "not again!" feeling. At the lost luggage office, he made another mental note to make yet another mental list of the things that a person with half a brain would not pack in his suitcase, in case this should happen again. And it inevitably would happen again.

This sort of crap always happened to him. The realization was painful: he was not and would never be one of the lucky ones. He would never win the lottery. His fate was to toil and sweat for everything he would ever get in his entire life.

He didn't want his mind wandering in that direction right now, there was too much work to do and time was short. He wanted to re-familiarize himself with the basic facts before he tried to interview anyone about them. Inside his three-ring binder, he had a selection of newspaper articles and photo-copied pages from various books on the subject.

The place of the first apparitions is known as Apparition Hill. It is situated just above the Bijakovo village of Podbrdo. A broad and steep footpath leads from the village up to the place of the apparitions. The once narrow and treacherous path is now broad and smooth, its edges softened by the millions of pilgrims who have come to the site. Half way up the path there is a massive plain wooden cross, where on the third day of the apparitions, June 26, 1981, The Blessed Virgin appeared to the visionary Marija Pavlovic.

The actual site where the apparitions are said to have taken place is a large barren space on a rocky plateau, nearly a hundred meters in diameter. At the exact spot where the visionaries claimed 'The Lady' had appeared to them, another tall cross is erected. It stands, planted into a large pile of stones.

To the millions of souls, sick, dying or filled with deep unquenchable spiritual hunger, this hill and this cross were Calvary itself. He read on.

According to the testimony of the six young visionaries, The Blessed Virgin has been appearing daily in Medjugorje since June 24, 1981. On that day the visionaries were frightened by the apparition and ran away. On the following day, June 25, they responded to Our Lady's call and went to Apparition Hill, where for the first time they prayed and spoke with her. That is why this day is celebrated as the anniversary of the apparitions of the Queen of Peace, as Our Lady introduced herself.

Tony paged through the notes until he came upon old black and white photos of the children. There was nothing special about them. They were simple folk in simple clothes, telling a story that was anything but simple. The words they used to describe the visions were childlike, immature, and unsophisticated. However, when they began to quote 'The Lady,' they suddenly developed the vocabulary of Rhodes Scholars. It was one more unexplainable fact in a series of baffling, inscrutable facts.

Tony picked up the photos of the six children and read the notes he'd jotted on the back of each.

Vicka Ivankovic-Mijatovic. She came from a family of eight children. Her prayer mission given to her by Our Lady was to pray for the sick. (Each of the visionaries claimed to have been given a specific "prayer mission" or group of people to pray for by The Blessed Virgin). The information that The Lady dictated to Vicka through the visions is contained in two hand written notebooks, which she will publish when Our Lady tells her the time is right. They allegedly contain the Blessed Virgin's life story, among other things.

Ivan Dragicevic. He is the older of the two boys who saw visions. His prayer mission given by Our Lady is to pray for priests, families, and the youth of the world.

Mirjana Dragicevic (no relation to Ivan). She is the lead and the most outspoken of all the children. Her prayer mission from Our Lady is to pray for all unbelievers.

Ivanka Ivankovic. The first to see Our Lady on June 24, 1981, and the youngest of the four girls. Her prayer mission from Our Lady is to pray for families.

Jakov Colo. The "baby" of the group. The youngest of the seers. His prayer mission given by Our Lady is to pray for the sick. He was key in terms of the authenticity of the apparitions. It was, for all intents and purposes, inconceivable that a healthy, ten-year-old Bosnian boy would prefer to spend three hours a day in prayer in a church than outside playing soccer with his friends.

Marija Pavlovic. Her prayer mission given by Our Lady is to pray for all the souls in purgatory. She is of particular interest because she claims to still see apparitions every day.

He had trouble keeping them separated in his mind—all the names sounded the same to him. He spread out the photos of the six children on the seat next to him. They didn't look particularly special in any way. In fact, in many ways, they were just like all the others.

Why did every visionary since the beginning of time seem to get secrets about the end of the world? Did the Holy Mother really think that Armageddon and the Apocalypse were kid-friendly topics? And could these six young country bumpkins really conspire to dupe the entire world? Were these the faces of brazen liars, shamelessly taking advantage of the poor and the sick? He shook his head and yawned. *We'll soon see!*

For this to be the least bit fruitful, he'd have to come away with a cool supernatural angle for his story. *That stuff was gold! The more mystical the mumbo-jumbo and the more cosmic the caca, the better. People eat up everything paranormal and arcane nowadays.* But, if there was something more to it—something he could even slightly believe—he might get some 'old-time-religion' himself and pray for his own miracle.

He looked back at the photos. All of the visionaries' versions of the vision were virtually the same, but not exactly the same. Frankly, that made it all the more believable to him. If they'd all spouted the exact same story, it would have seemed too rehearsed.

It wasn't until he'd seen the video of the children *en medias-vision*—oblivious to the hundreds of flashbulbs going off around, seemingly lost in another world—that he'd even considered there might be something more to all this. There was a wondrous, almost jaw-dropping, look of perfect bliss on their faces as they received their messages. There was nothing scandalous or tawdry in their appearance or behavior, nothing to suggest that they were anything but what they appeared to be, a bunch of shit-poor peasants saying their prayers.

However, they were not like the others he'd met in Bosnia. They appeared to have a solid sense of inner peace that was virtually absent from anyone in this country. The folks he'd met were haunted in every sense of the word, and each one of them seemed to walk the earth accompanied by ghosts and guilt from a past that none of them could forget or move on from in any meaningful way. Where he heard thunder, they heard artillery. Where he heard the milk man making his early morning delivery, they heard ghostly horsemen in the night. Tony strongly suspected that every single adult he'd met on the trip was suffering from PTSD to one degree or another. The depth of their hurt in most cases went far beyond their capacity to either comprehend or deal with. At first glance, they all appeared perfectly normal, going about their daily business. But just below the surface, they were walking a tightrope, never fully free from a deep, corroding sense of helplessness. It was no surprise that a sense of despair hung thick in the air. It was sad and more than a little bit frightening, because no matter where he went, it felt like a volcano was simmering just below the surface, waiting to blow.

He was exhausted and needed to sleep; he hadn't slept well on the entire trip.

He thought of the people on the bus with him and considered the dread with which they must face sleep every night, the demons and the nightmares of war that filled the darkness each night as they reluctantly reached over to turn out the lights. Tony couldn't fathom the depths of these wounds. In any event, right now, he didn't have the time.

The bus hit a bump and he grabbed the armrest as if he were on a plane in turbulence. There was a pronounced difference in the quality and upkeep of the roads between Croatia and Bosnia. Croatia appeared to be building modern superhighways everywhere one looked, while many of the Bosnian roads were still pitted and pockmarked from shelling that happened over a decade ago. He guessed that Croatia's one thousand miles of spectacular beaches provided the revenue for major public works. Bosnia was pretty much land-locked and the tourists, he suspected, were still too afraid of the land mine situation to return in earnest. He glanced out the window and a magnificent sight caught his eye. In the distance, the storm clouds had begun to separate and a spectacular shaft of golden light had broken through the dark canopy of clouds, probing the hillside below it and illuminating the rustic old stone houses built into the hill.

The grumpy, white-haired guy in the shabby suit, sitting opposite him, sneezed loudly. Tony politely said *"Gesundheit."* But the cranky curmudgeon merely stifled a brief but clearly disgusted laugh in response. The very brief conversation Tony had earlier with him at the bus station revealed almost nothing about the fellow except his obvious disdain for Americans. That did not make him special in these parts. Long before the Dayton Accords were signed, ostensibly ending the war, all three sides – Serbs, Bosnians and Croats - had vilified America, first for its inaction and then for its action.

At the time the war was raging, Tony had been a promising young filmmaker just out of UCLA Film School, spending most of his days lying on a beach and most of his nights chasing women. He'd actually double-majored, psychology being his other area of concentration, but that degree had died from neglect a long time ago.

His first film had managed to get shown in a number of festivals to very positive notices and he thought he was well on his way to a major career. His life seemed to stretch before him in an endless glow of possibility and he fully expected to be successful for all his days. At least that was how he chose to remember it. In reality, it may not have been as perfectly idyllic as all that, and the habit of thinking it so only further illustrated the contrast between the promise of his halcyon days and the frustration and disappointment of his current situation.

Unfortunately, he was an artist in a world of accountants, an idealist among pragmatists, and the killer instinct was never something he'd possessed. However, in Los Angeles, it was practically a prerequisite. It seemed impossible for anyone to get anywhere in the movie business of that period. For every filmmaker that saw even a modicum of success, legions more were doomed to remain groveling, obsequious drones. The only way to break from this uncouth and uncultured treadmill was to abandon it altogether and start over fresh somewhere else.

At forty-five, he was too old to be a young talent anymore, but he still felt like his career was only just beginning. This project would be the one that would finally put him on the map; finally make all things right for him and Claire. He was counting on it. He was more than counting on it.

CHAPTER 2

THE PILGRIMS

Thursday, 2:45pm

The cantankerous, white-haired guy refused to even tell Tony his name when they had spoken earlier. This guy was sent directly from central casting: eastern-European, overweight, bad teeth, marginal knowledge of personal hygiene.

He was probably about sixty but it was hard to tell; his piercing blue eyes had seen a lot in just a few years and some folks weathered the experience better than others. He was also the only person on the bus wearing a jacket and tie, and Tony guessed he was a professional of some kind who wanted to make that fact abundantly clear to everyone. Although he possessed a quiet dignity, there was something about his manner, a brusqueness that suggested he'd spent a great deal of time operating in a far lower social stratum than his clothing might have indicated. This was a man who clearly didn't like being challenged; as evidenced by the way his entire frame swelled up like a cornered cat, when Tony asked him about his line of work. His command of English was impressive, as was that of most everyone Tony had met, a fact that he had not expected. In fact, the bus he was riding on had a total of five passengers, a driver and his assistant and all of them spoke reasonably good English. This was especially surprising because you could not have asked for a more radically diverse bunch. The guy's most striking physical feature, in Tony's view, was his bulbous red nose and cheeks ripe with broken capillaries. Tony was well acquainted with the condition. Had it not been for Claire's intervention, he might share that same affliction.

When he first met Claire, Tony thought of himself as quite the Hollywood hotshot. The one thing he never viewed himself as was an addict. Addicts were unsympathetic and unworthy. They were selfish and inconsiderate. He had his life firmly under control.

"Ha!" he laughed out loud at the thought, startling the surly guy in the suit, who gave him yet another disdainful grimace.

When things really fell apart, Tony could not have been more alone. He had no family, no really close friends, no support structure of any kind. But he had Claire.

He had lied to all his friends, stolen from them to feed his habit, and when it all went to hell, he didn't have the courage to ask them for forgiveness, let alone ask for help. Claire was the only constant in his life; she'd been there for the whole ride. She had gotten used to his wild mood swings, the soaring flights of hope one day and the abject despair the next.

He bitterly regretted the lies. He had abused the goodness and the trust of the people he loved the most. He begged Claire for forgiveness, telling her that the drugs were just a temporary way to fight off the impatience and frustration at his slow progress—never mentioning his growing fears about the bleak-looking years that lay ahead.

She never judged him and never felt there was anything to forgive. She was just there. She never told him that he had 'nobody to blame but himself' or 'you brought all this on yourself' or 'you made your bed, now you've got to sleep in it.' She never gave him any advice at all, probably because she knew him well enough to recognize that taking advice was not one of his virtues.

He had to make things right with her. *Nothing* else mattered. If this trip so far had taught him nothing else, it had taught him that.

He stretched and looked around. On the last seat in the back was a young guy, possibly in his late twenties, very bookish-looking. Tony pegged him as a student; he had that timid scholarly look about him. He reminded Tony of a guy he used to score coke from in Santa Monica years ago in a different lifetime. Although he wore nothing to suggest it, Tony suspected he was a Muslim, not a great stretch considering eighty percent of the country was Muslim. But, there was something in the kid's eyes as he watched Tony speak to the white-haired guy; something that Tony found disconcerting, something that no amount of fake smiles and pleasant words could mask: hatred.

At first, the kid seemed terrified and afraid when Tony approached him and started a conversation, but after a few minutes he let his guard down and chatted amiably. He wasn't actually as introverted and timid as he appeared, he was merely being cautious and circumspect. Tony's initial assumption was correct, his name was Amir and he was a student, from the University in Sarajevo. He'd made a brief stop in Mostar to take some pictures of the famous Mostar Bridge for his photography class. Tony had visited the renowned bridge too, but was only mildly impressed. For some reason he'd expected it to be much grander. The show put on by local divers was amazing and far more entertaining in his view. Yet it was the story of the bridge and what it represented rather than its physical appearance that was really incredible, and emblematic of the entire conflict.

Built in the middle ages out of limestone, the high-arching bridge represented the cross roads of the Ottoman Empire with the west and for over six centuries, Catholics, Muslims, Orthodox Christian, and even a small Jewish population lived in complete harmony there. Obviously, it all changed in 1992 with the war. And the bridge, a marvel of antiquity, was shelled by Croat artillery until it was completely destroyed.

After the war, the remarkable divers along with the townsfolk actually fished out all of the stones from the bottom of the river and completely rebuilt the bridge. It was an astounding feat; a massive jigsaw puzzle, but in every way, a true labor of love. It spoke volumes about the people living there. Mostar, like every Bosnian town he'd visited, was brimming with all the usual suspects one encounters in times of war or shortly thereafter. There were the sketchy-looking characters, blending into the background, whose shadowy presence and purpose was largely unknown, but it almost inevitably had something to do with the black market or spying for the government.

Tony was lucky enough to be present the day they reopened the bridge in 2004 and the show the divers put on was awe-inspiring. They continued the age old tradition of diving carrying multiple torches through the air with them, and the effect against the night sky was breathtaking. This was what he wanted to see more of! He wanted stories of resilience and heroic deeds in the face of insurmountable odds. These were the kind of stories that would make his film jump off the screen!

He looked at the young Muslim in the back of the bus and wondered what remarkable tale he might have to tell if Tony could ever get him to open up. Like the rest of "the pilgrims," he got on the bus in Mostar and was on his way to Medjugorje, the place of the miracles.

Instinctively, Tony liked him; thinking that once you got past his thick paranoid outer layer (which virtually everyone seemed to possess in this part of the world) he was probably just like any American college kid; overwhelmed with school work while simultaneously worrying about finding a job thereafter to pay off his education. Well, at least in this semi-socialist environment he won't have the kind of crushing student loans that American kids were currently burdened with. More importantly, he was inquisitive, and Tony immediately sensed that the kid might be helpful with his project.

Reaching up to get a bottle of water from his bag in the overhead compartment, Tony felt the eyes of the "professor," as he called him, observing closely. Sure enough, he was correct, the guy, sitting behind Tony to the right, was staring at him with a quizzical look on his face, as if he was desperately trying to figure Tony out. This guy was cut from a different cloth altogether. While most of the Balkan folks he'd encountered were intensely private and generally disinterested in other people, this one seemed to be watching Tony's every move like a hawk since they got on the bus in Mostar. He was easily the oldest in the group and looked like an old rabbinical scholar, which Tony doubted very much that they had around here. Nonetheless, the unkempt beard and the little half-y spectacles gave him a look of a wise old wizard from some fantasy novel. The fidgety and high-strung professor looked perpetually flustered, and when Tony first got up from his seat to venture to the back of the bus, the old man watched him every step of the way, without being covert about it at all. When Tony returned to his seat, he was met with a grim and haughty look of disapproval.

Whereas the white-haired guy in the suit seemed to prefer yelling every word he said, this guy spoke softly, with a voice that conveyed total conviction, although his supercilious grin was omnipresent. There would be no point trying to talk to him; Tony had seen his type before and wasn't going to waste his breath. It annoyed him because the old man certainly had the look of a wise old sage, and Tony really could use such knowledge for his research; it might prove a great time-saver, as he was approaching the end of the trip and his mission was nowhere near complete. At the rest stop he was determined to try and get them all to talk. He hoped that if one started, the rest would follow.

Suddenly, someone clearing his throat with great zealousness caught Tony's attention. It was the Croat kid, sitting in front of him. He had headphones on and was blissfully unaware of how loud he was. Earlier in the trip, he thoughtlessly reclined his seat back all the way, whacking Tony across the knees. Tony gently, but repeatedly, bumped the back of the kid's seat until he got the message and moved it forward a bit. Tony guessed that he was in his mid-to-late twenties, but he couldn't be sure. One thing he was sure of, though, was that this young Croatian kid would be the key to his plan, his oracle. In the bus station, Tony noticed the kid loved to talk, albeit mostly about himself, but that didn't matter. As long as he got the conversation started, Tony was sure he would rope the rest in. That was the way to make real progress; to get the kind of extemporaneous banter that made for great dialogue. He realized that his script was still stiff as a board and desperately needed an injection of some fresh local color to spruce it up, and the menacing-looking guy with the tats and the ponytail might do the trick.

The Croat looked like a young, muscle-bound, Robert DeNiro. He was fascinated to learn that Tony was a real Hollywood director and asked if he would put him in his next movie. Once the kid had asked that, Tony knew he had him. Still, he had to be careful, because this guy looked dangerous, really dangerous. From his slave tattoos, to his short tight pony tail revealing a nasty looking scar on his neck, this one looked like he really enjoyed mixing it up, and Tony had no desire to set him off.

The Croat was also important because he was probably the only Catholic in their group and Tony was having a hard time finding any information on the church's stance on the visions. In fact, the last item he could find on the internet was so old it still referred to the region as Yugoslavia!

The latest comments on Medjugorje from the Catholic Bishops of the Socialist Federal Republics of Yugoslavia are consistent with the country's established practice of authentic ecclesiastical prudence. It demonstrates that the Church respects facts above all, that it carefully measures its competence and that in all matters it is mostly concerned for the spiritual welfare of the faithful.

A quotation from the Committee of Bishops in 1993 was the most recent comment he could find and it provided little insight to the Church's position:

"We bishops, after a three-year-long commission study accept Medjugorje as a holy place, as a shrine. This means that we have nothing against it if someone venerates the Mother of God in a manner also in agreement with the teaching and belief of the Church. Therefore, we are leaving that to further study. The Church does not rush."

Tony closed the notebook and put it away. Despite his lack of knowledge on the maneuverings of the Catholic Church, he had always found their handling of such situations as overly esoteric, and this was no exception. They were virtually saying: "No comment." Surely, he thought, the local Catholic population could light a candle to that mystery.

The driver's assistant stood up and pulled a microphone off the wall, but before he spoke, he reached into his inside jacket pocket and removed a small metallic device which he pressed against his throat.

"Dvije minute do odmorisa," he said with the aid of his vocal resonator. The war hadn't gotten him, it was the old vice: nicotine.

"Two minutes to rest stop. We stay twenty minutes." Then he repeated the announcement again in Bosnian before putting back the mic and sitting back down across from the driver.

At first, Tony was confused as hell when he saw the bus had an assistant driver, who appeared to serve no function other than ticket taker and occasional tour guide—things that the driver could undoubtedly do by himself. It was when he took out the voice assisting device that Tony was convinced he'd stepped into a Fellini movie!

Luckily, the young Muslim kid educated him on the subject.

"After the war, most of our train lines were destroyed and the government had no money to rebuild them. So, long distance bus lines became the primary means of travel, near and far. Each bus had two drivers because the first driver will drive to the destination and the assistant will drive on the return trip, while the other sleeps. They don't waste time taking tickets when you board. You leave at exactly the appointed time and then the assistant collects the tickets during the ride. Much more efficient."

When put that way, it seemed to make perfect sense, as had most of the peculiarities he'd come across on the trip, once they'd been explained. Simple things like not wearing your shoes indoors (you want to walk on your carpet with shoes that have walked in dog shit and piss all day?), warming the milk before you put it in your coffee, etc. These were tidbits he'd only just learned but immediately knew that he'd be doing for the rest of his life.

As the rain howled against the bus windows, Tony decided to try to meditate for five minutes before they reached their stop. Before doing so, he wanted to grab a couple of quick pictures of the interior of the bus. He walked to the front of the bus and looking backwards took a flash photo of the interior. The flash was met by a mass of angry faces, including the old "professor" who got right in Tony's face and demanded to see the photo. Tony obliged him, although he couldn't understand the level of hostility. When the old man was satisfied, he sat back down, continuing to grumble.

This wasn't going to be easy. He needed to gain their trust. For that to happen, there was one thing he needed to do.

Tony smiled to himself and plopped back into his seat. As he gently let his eyelids close, he began to feel the bus slowing down and turning. Sleepy eyes glanced out the window and through the rainy pane he could see an old adorable little structure that looked to him a bit like a Vale Colorado Ski Chalet. It made him smile but he quickly regarded it with increasingly detached attention.

Something was nagging at him as he reached to turn up his jacket collar, something that he couldn't quite put his finger on. He was flat broke. The thought haunted him constantly, rarely giving him a moment's peace. The grant money was an unanticipated life line which he knew would only come once. But he also knew it was neither an amnesty nor an absolution from the past—it was merely a deferment, a postponement of the inevitable. Now he needed to make things happen. If this plan didn't work…well, it had to work.

He looked out the window again and regarded the darkening sky and the fading landscape. Why here? There were any number of reasons or no reason whatsoever why the Blessed Virgin might have picked these particular children. His memory was already overloaded with facts, faces, and names. What was it about Medjugorie? And how was it possible that nobody in Hollywood had thought to do a movie about this place yet? He could not believe his good fortune on the count. But the clock was ticking.

He glanced at his watch and turned on the stop-watch function. He set it to count down from twenty four hours. This morning when he awoke, he had made a decision. If he couldn't get all the information he needed, or at least a spark to keep the flame of the project alive, in the next twenty four hours…then there was little point…in anything. He was tired of being a failure, tired of being a burden to everyone. He had nothing to go home for if he went home empty handed. So, why go home? Why go anywhere? If he came back empty, Claire would be done with him, forever. And he was willing to do anything to prevent that from happening. Anything. If he failed…he knew he wouldn't be going back. Twenty four hours. With a troubled but tired mind, he yawned, closed his eyes, and in a second, drifted into the arms of Morpheus.

CHAPTER 3

THE OASIS

Thursday, 3:00pm

The bus pulled up right in front of the rest area and stopped. The driver exited first, followed by his assistant. The other four pilgrims followed and one by one took out their cigarettes and lit up. Apparently, going without food, water, and a bathroom for several hours had been a breeze compared to the nicotine withdrawal.

They entered the rest stop and the driver promptly headed for the mens room. The small dining area had four small squares of old cigarette stained Formica. There was a small bar and a glass case full of various cakes and pastries. Next to that stood a small counter with a big old cash register on it. An old-fashioned cigarette machine, the kind which you pull the handles, was against the far wall, with a dingy sign reading: "Ronhill." In the farthest corner stood a small statue of the Madonna holding the baby Jesus in her arms. In front of the icon was a red candle and a small bouquet of fresh flowers.

From behind the counter, the smell of strong coffee wafted. There was a small grill but nothing was cooking on it. A tired-looking old man stood behind the counter. If he'd noticed their arrival, he gave no outward sign of it.

The bus driver reemerged from the bathroom and promptly said: "Twenty minutes, then we go. Don't be late." Then he lit another cigarette and walked over to the counter. The old man already had coffee ready for him. They nodded at each other without saying a word or exchanging any payment; clearly a routine established long ago.

The professional-looking guy, the one in the suit, walked over to the counter, shaking the rain off his jacket. He looked at the case of not-quite-fresh baked goods and shook his head.

The two younger pilgrims, the Bosnian and the Croat, sat together at a table and began to look through the newspapers as they continued to smoke.

The bus driver walked over to another table and sat down with his coffee. Yawning, he absently pointed with his thumb over his shoulder.

"Oh, yeah, by the way, the bathrooms are over there, down the hall. Just make sure you hold down the handle when you flush."

"Don't worry. I wouldn't take a dump in this country," said the man in the suit, with unvarnished disgust.

The student, Amir, grit his teeth and quietly said to the Croat: "That explains why he's so full of shit."

"What do you mean?" asked the Croat.

"Never mind," said Amir.

The man in the suit stood at the counter and gazed around with a dour look on his face.

"So, what do you have to eat?" he asked.

The old man barely moved and merely pointed to the menu on the wall without saying anything. The guy in the suit squinted at it.

The driver's assistant came in from outside and shook his umbrella. He placed it on a table and walked over to the counter. He whistled to get the old man's attention. He then pointed to the cigarettes on the wall behind him. The old man slid a pack across the counter top and the assistant dropped a few coins down. He lit a cigarette while still standing at the counter and took a deep, pleasurable, drag. He exhaled, and satisfied, he walked away and sat down next to the driver.

"You forgot your change," said the old man.

The assistant pulled out his voice articulator and spoke.

"Keep it."

The old man put the change in his pocket and almost smiled.

"Do you have any *real* food?" asked the man in the suit.

This time, the old man looked directly at him, paused, then pointed to the menu again.

"I see," he continued. "I will ask you again: Do you have any *real* food? Not this stale shit in cellophane?"

"No," answered the old man.

"And why not?"

"Because nobody stays more than fifteen minutes and there's no time to eat real food," said the old man in tones of shallow indifference.

The two younger men laughed out loud, as if they had won some small victory. The man in the suit grabbed a small loaf of bread and a cup of coffee and threw some coins disdainfully down on the counter. He turned and walked over to sit at a table by himself. After taking a bite of bread and sipping his coffee, he looked over at the Bosnian.

"So, where is your idiot friend?" he asked.

"He's not my friend."

"You were talking to him."

"If you paid attention you'd have noticed, I wasn't talking, I was listening."

"Yeah. Pretty much all you can do with a guy like that," added the Croatian with a laugh.

"He would try the patience of Job, that one," said the professor. "I wonder if he's married?"

"I believe he said he was, somewhere in the middle of reading us his resume...the second time," said the man in the suit, with a mouthful of bread.

"Why don't you ask him?" said the student. "I'm sure you two have a lot in common."

The man in the suit spit out a piece of bread. "I don't like smart mouthed kids."

"Good. Then the feeling is mutual."

"So, where is he anyway?" asked the Croat.

"Who cares?" replied the professor as he walked toward the rest room. "Probably asleep on the bus. He must be exhausted from all that talking. He hasn't shut up since he got on in Mostar." He disappeared down the hallway toward the rest rooms.

After giving a moment or two of consideration, the Croat looked around and weakly suggested, "Do you think we should wake him?"

"No!" was blasted back at him in unison.

Back on the bus, Tony yawned and through sleepy eyes glanced at his watch. He then stretched and looked around to discover he was alone. For a brief moment, he was terrified then he calmed down when he looked through the window and saw the rest stop. He stood up and put on his jacket, every muscle in his body ached. He used to be fresh as a daisy after a nap, now it always made him feel like he had the flu. He had to shake it off quickly, because the clock was ticking. As he headed out the door of the bus, he made sure to take out his camera, because this place looked priceless. Then he remembered; the camera was in his suitcase, which was lost in Croatia somewhere. He pulled the cheap little Fuji digital camera, which he'd purchased in the airport gift shop, out of his bag—it was better than nothing.

As he stepped off the bus, he was immediately struck by the resounding quiet of the place. He looked around and couldn't even hear a bird. What a difference from the cities he'd visited in the country, with their cacophony of cars honking their horns. Not to be outdone by the cars, the drivers of carts yelled at the top of their voices. Of course, every cafe had to have ethnic music blaring out of cheap radios and the street vendors felt compelled to call out to absolutely every possible customer.

This place was another world altogether. The smell of the freshly rain-soaked forest was intoxicating as well. He felt so invigorated he almost forgot his screaming bladder.

Inside the rest stop, the pilgrims smoked and read their papers in silence. Of course, the silence was broken the moment Tony burst through the door.

"Whoa! What happened? I dosed off for a sec and when I came to, I was all alone! I'm like, where'd everybody go?"

He hated the words as soon as they came out. He was trying too hard. He needed to dial it back a bit.

The Croat said to the student, "It's really amazing, even when he's alone, he's still talking."

"Shit, my neck hurts," Tony said massaging his neck and shoulders. "I must have slept on it funny."

"I understand silence is very effective cure for that," said the man in the suit.

"Funny! So, where are we?" Tony asked. "Seriously, where are we?"

Silence.

"Come on, you all speak English, we already established that."

"Apparently our first mistake," said the student.

"Yeah, no kiddin'! It took me an hour to get a peep out of any of you!" Tony laughed, ignoring the insult or missing it entirely.

"It seems some people just can't take a hint," said the man in the suit.

Words began to form on Tony's lips, witty, clever, caustic words, but he thought better of it and decided to let that one slide as well as he wandered around the dining area.

He nodded politely to the old man behind the counter, who hardly noticed. The old man was also right out of central casting: "shopkeeper, Eastern Europe." He had high sharp cheekbones and a weak chin. His broad forehead glistened with perspiration that he felt no obligation to wipe away.

The edges of all the tables had stains from burned down cigarettes, as did the counter, as did the window ledges. Suddenly, his eyes stopped on the cigarette vending machine.

"Oh my God! I haven't seen one of these things in ages!" He took out his camera and started snapping pictures as if it were a holy relic. He walked over and started pulling on the knobs as if it were a toy.

The rest stop was clearly the work of a master craftsman, albeit, a master craftsman from a hundred years ago. The walls and the ceilings were braced and lined with powerful-looking split logs, probably oak, judging by the grain. The walls were stucco, probably covering cinderblocks. Only the floor seemed out of place. It was cheap, dingy, yellowing linoleum, probably circa 1960. It was covered with stains and the requisite cigarette burns.

Tony thought about his own powers of observation; they were very acute. He considered for a second that he might have made a fine detective had he not thrown his life away chasing a career in Hollywood.

The professor stepped out of the bathroom, eyeballed Tony holding his camera, then turned around and went back inside. Tony paid him no mind and continued his photo essay of the cigarette machine.

A small black metal electric fan sat on top of the cigarette machine, spinning slowly and doing absolutely nothing to circulate the air. It could have been a Hollywood prop, something out of an old black and while film noir, or an old Spencer Tracy movie about a hard boiled journalist, or a courtroom drama in the hot south.

Next to the fan stood a small plastic statuette of the Virgin Mary. Tony fully expected to find her imagery everywhere in these parts.

A moment later, the professor reemerged, hoping the coast was clear, but Tony pounced and immediately flashed a picture of him. The flash nearly gave him a heart attack!

"Jesus! Must you do that?" he yelled, grabbing his chest.

Tony threw both hands up.

"Sorry! My bad! Won't do it again! But this place is priceless! I'll bet it hasn't changed in ages. But seriously now, where are we?"

"Herzegovina," muttered the bus driver.

Tony smiled, "Obviously, we're in—wait! Where? I thought we were in Bosnia!"

Yawning, the bus driver said, "Relax! It is Bosnia!"

Tony felt like he'd been punked. "Don't do that to me! I'm on a tight schedule here."

The man in the suit turned around and looked at Tony in bewildered disbelief.

"You are on a tight schedule and you are taking Bosnian public transportation?" He burst out laughing. The Croat started laughing too, but Amir, the Bosnian, threw him a look of contempt.

"What are *you* laughing about? As if Croatian buses are any better?"

The man in the suit patted Tony on the back.

"Relax, your virgin isn't going anywhere."

"But I am," Tony said. "And after seeing the Virgin, I'm on the last bus out tomorrow night to Split. And after Split, it's *Zay*-dar."

"Za-dar. Soft a," said the Croatian.

"Ok. Cool. Then a quick flight to Za-*greb* and I'll have seen the entire country."

They all exchange confused looks.

"Which country?" Amir asked.

"The former Yugoslavia," Tony replied matter-of-factly.

Almost in harmony, they all groaned at the remark.

"Lemme tell ya," Tony added. "You sure have some gorgeous countryside here. I mean, if this were America, the whole country would be a National Park. Wish I had time to see more, but I gotta get home and finish the research for my film."

The bus driver looked up from his newspaper at Tony, who was looking at his watch again.

"What kind of film?" asked the driver.

Tony pretended to almost miss the question.

"Huh? Oh. Well, I'm here doing research for a film about the war."

More groans, but this time they were suspicious groans, groans laced with inquisitiveness. As Tony had hoped, the comment hit the mark and all eyes were on him.

"Another apologetic American documentary, no doubt," said the man in the suit.

"Another exploitative: "We must let the world know what happened here," bullshit American movie?" asked Amir.

Tony stood up and slowly waltzed across the room.

"Nope! In fact, I doubt there's ever been a film like this one. You've obviously seen all those awful films about Bosnia, like "Welcome to Sarajevo," "Harrison's Flowers"?"

"No Man's Land?" added Amir.

"What?" asked Tony.

"No Man's Land? Another film about the war?"

Tony squinted and searched his memory, "Nope. Missed that one."

"For God's sake, it won the Oscar! What kind of filmmaker are you?" thundered the professor.

Tony was unmoved.

"I don't really follow commercial films. I'm interested in foreign films, strictly art house stuff."

"It was a Bosnian film," said Amir with mild disdain.

Tony sensed he was losing them. Apparently this film was important to them. He'd make it right, but not now. Now, it would seem like he was just placating them. He decided he'd try and get them talking about movies, everybody loved movies. But before he could, the young Muslim broke in.

"Why do you want to make a movie about us anyway?" asked Amir.

Perfect, Tony thought. He couldn't have asked for a better setup.

"Well," said Tony. "You see, I was talking to this friend of mine in New York who told me about this human-rights slash humanitarian organization that runs these volunteer groups into Bosnia every summer to work at an orphanage. They look for volunteers to take the trip and work with the kids. They're really just like glorified camp counselors, they teach 'em to read and to swim and to play soccer and stuff like that."

"Americans teaching Bosnians to play soccer!" said the Croat. "That's good one!"

"Then you speak Bosnian?" asked the professor.

"No, no, no," said Tony.

The professor rolled his eyes.

"Then how, pray tell, do you teach them to read?"

"I don't," said Tony. "Other guys do. Teachers. English teachers. Besides we have translators. And every volunteer teaches them a bit about their own particular skill."

"And you think war orphans need to learn how to make movies?" asked Amir.

"I teach 'em basic acting skills. But it's more than that. It teaches them to work hard and to concentrate and the importance of teamwork. But most importantly, it builds confidence in the kids." The faces he saw were unimpressed. "Anyway, you've got theaters, you make movies right? Somebody's got to act in them!"

Silence followed for a minute or two as the American's thought process sank in. The man in the suit stood up, walked over toward Tony, then stopped and faced the rest of them. He gestured toward Tony as he spoke.

"And *these* people lead the free world!"

Tony kept right on going.

"And I thought it would be a great place to do research for my film. I could interview the kids about their war experiences. Real first-hand stuff. Practically a reality show!"

"You really think that is in the children's best interest?" asked Amir.

"Absolutely! Seriously, any shrink will tell you, it's healthy to talk about your problems, get 'em out in the open. They say 'if you can name it, you can tame it!' What do your shrinks here in Bosnia say?"

"We don't have shrinks," said Amir.

"What's a shrink?" asked the Croat.

"A psychiatrist," bellowed the man in the suit. "And we do not have them here because we do not need them here. The Slavic people are cut from a victorious stock. We do not whine about our feelings to total strangers and then pay them for the privilege."

Tony was stunned.

"No shrinks? Wow. I've been seeing a shrink since I was fifteen."

"And it's clearly done wonders for you," said the professor. "But, let me correct that statement. It's not exactly true that we have no psychologists."

"Ha! I knew it!"

"We have one."

"In your town?"

"In our country. And he's in Ljubljana."

"Gesundheit," said Tony as he walked around the perimeter of the room, scratching his head. This little tidbit actually made a lot of sense to him.

"You know," he said absently, "maybe if you had more shrinks, you barbarians wouldn't go around killing each other all the time."

Before he'd even finished the sentence he knew it was a mistake. Instantly, the Croat was at his throat.

"Shut the fuck up! Who are you to tell us anything!" yelled the Croat in fury, throwing him against the wall. Amir and the professor rushed in and separated them.

"Whoa! Jesus! What did I say?" said Tony catching his breath. "Try decaf, pal! And maybe some mouthwash while you're at it!"

The professor looked the Croat in the eye and spoke in calming tones.

"Take it easy! We'll be back on the bus in just a few minutes and you won't have to listen to him anymore."

Gradually, tempers calmed and everyone sat back down, except the Croat who walked over to the window and lit another cigarette.

"Fucking Americans," he muttered.

The driver, who had made no effort at all to stop the ruckus, smiled and took out a small transistor radio and headphones. Apparently, it took more than a simple bar fight to impress him.

Amir walked over to the Croat and both stood silently watching the rain. The professor joined them a moment later.

"I travel to America often," he said. "They're not all like this one."

Tony, still angry about what he considered an unprovoked attack, decided to put it aside for the good of his project. This seemed like a pretty good time to try and apologize and make light of the matter.

"Look, I was just making conversation. No harm, no foul. OK?"

He extended a hand in an offering of peace, but the Croat just slapped it away.

"Fine, be that way. Can't say I didn't try."

As he spoke, Tony noticed a nasty looking scar on the Croat's neck, not the kind you got by cutting yourself shaving. He tried to reach out again in an even more thoughtful voice.

"Hey, that's some scar you got there. How?"

The Croat spun around in a fury but stopped himself before he raised his hands. He relaxed and walked away.

"I am done talking to you," he said, walking over to the counter and ordering coffee, *"Kavu, molim. Hvala vam." Coffee please. Thanks.*

If there was such a thing as "angry silence," that would have accurately described the atmosphere. Tony realized that he'd just gotten a crash course in the unique east-central European view of the world. This was a world where WWII was won by the Russians, not by the Americans. Where a Croatian-born, Serbian-raised man named Tito had not only defeated Hitler, but had kept the USSR out of Yugoslavia for half a century. It was nothing that an American would ever learn about in his history books. He made a mental note of it.

Tony sat at a table which had a large burn spot on its corner, obviously from an unwatched cigarette that had burned all the way down.

"It's a miracle this whole place hasn't burned down," he muttered softly.

"It can't," said the Croat.

Tony didn't realize he'd spoken loud enough to be heard, but evidently he had.

"Why not?" he asked.

"It's made of stone. All of the houses here are made of brick or stone."

Tony motioned to the massive wooden column in the walls.

"What about those?"

The Croat yawned.

"They're only decorative. Probably plastic."

Tony walked over and rapped his fist on one and nearly dented it.

"Well, I'll be..." he said.

"I hear from my second cousin, who lives in Chicago, that in America, all the houses are made of wood. Is that true?" said the Croat.

"I wouldn't say *all* of them, but yes, a fair number are."

"How do they stand? Wouldn't the first strong wind knock them down? And don't you have big tornadoes in America?"

"It's the way they're built that makes them stand. Their strength lies in the engineering, not the materials used to build."

The Croat gave him a derisive smirk and turned away.

"You can have your engineering. I'll stick with my bricks and stones."

Tony sighed and glanced over at the bar, where the white-haired guy in the suit was staring at the professor, looking him over, in what appeared to be a supremely distrustful manner.

In an atypical gesture, the guy in the suit walked over to the professor, initiating a conversation, which to the untrained-in-Balkan-ways ear might have sounded more like an interrogation.

"Why do you travel to America so frequently?" he asked.

The professor put a hand to his ear as if he didn't hear him.

"You said you travel to America often and I was wondering why?"

The professor stepped back and considered the man in the suit for a moment, sizing him up.

"Not that it is any of your business, but I am...a professor," he said in guarded tones.

At hearing this, Amir's head spun and he turned and walked over to them.

"Really?" he asked. "What kind of professor?"

Tony noticed a tiny bead of sweat began to form on the professor's forehead. He suspected the old guy did not want to engage in any conversation about himself.

"History. I'm going to Medjugorje for a research study."

"Really?" said Tony, now also interested. "Hey, that's awesome! You can help with the accuracy of my script!"

"Oye ve!" muttered the professor under his breath, but the remark did not go unnoticed.

"Oye ve?" said the man in the suit. "What are you, a Jew?"

The professor took a deep breath, walked up to the man in the suit and looked him in the eye.

"I am not. But if I were, would it matter to you?"

Amir laughed.

"Not at all! *They* are equal opportunity murderers."

"I'm getting tired of your smart mouth," snarled the man in the suit. "Especially when no greater murderers have ever lived than your people! Or don't you know your own history?"

"You know nothing of my history, you Serb pig."

Veins bulged from the old guy's neck.

"I know a Serb civilian who was captured by Muslims, and skewered on a spear like a pig, then left to rot for all to see. He lived for days in unspeakable agony before he died."

"Yeah, yeah, yeah, that story's been around forever. It's bullshit Chetnik propaganda! And trust me, you don't want to start trading horror stories with me!"

Tony couldn't believe his luck. This was exactly the kind of exchange he expected to hear; he only wished he could take out his pocket recorder and tape it. He thought for the moment it was best that he remained the peacemaker.

"Chill out, guys!" he said. "We're all friends here, right?"

"No!"

"OK, but, we're all headed to Medjugorje, right? And it's the same thing that brought us all here, right?"

"Yes," said the Croat. "A bus."

"No, no, no," said Tony.

"Yes! It's right there. I can see it!"

Tony stood and stared in amazement at the Croat for a moment.

"No, no, I mean the reasons why we're here," Tony said.

"Oh," said the Croat. "That's not what you said."

"Sorry, I'll try to be more specific. Anyway, we're all headed to Medjugorje for the visions, right? We're all going to the site of the visions, to see Mirjana tomorrow, right?"

"Is there any other reason to go there?" the Croat sarcastically asked.

Tony honestly didn't know the answer. "That's a good question. I'll ask the driver."

He walked over to the driver who was sipping coffee while reading a newspaper with his earphones still on.

"So, tell us: is there any other reason to visit Medjugorje? Other than the obvious?"

The driver glanced up at Tony and with an annoyed look, took out the ear piece and whistled. Like a trained retriever, his assistant brought him a laminated card. He yawned and slowly began to read.

"Medjugorje is located in western Herzegovina close to the border of Croatia. It's best known for apparitions of the Blessed Virgin Mary which appeared to six children since 24 June 1981—see reference, blah, blah, blah.... It's now visited by pilgrims from around the entire world as a shrine. The name Medjugorje means the area "between the mountains." At an altitude of 200 meters above sea level, it has a mild Mediterranean climate."

He paused for a moment and cleared his throat, then continued in a far more dramatic voice.

"On the afternoon of June 24, 1981, two girls, Ivanka Ivankovic age 15, and Mirjana Dragicevic age 16, were returning home from a walk. As they passed a hill called Crnica, Ivanka saw a bright silhouette of a woman. She said to Mirjana, "It is the Gospa!" Our Lady. On June 25, the two girls returned to the hill with four others. Their names are, Vicka Ivankovic age 16, Ivan Dragicevic age 16, Maria Pavlovic age 16, and Jakov Colo age 10. The figure in white beckoned to them. The Lady, who calls herself the Queen of Peace, gave messages to them. To date, she has left thousands of messages. For the past several years, they come on the 25th of each month. There are six primary messages: conversion, prayer, fasting, faith, peace, and reconciliation."

He then looked up from the card and continued. This was clearly something he'd read countless time and had committed to memory. He looked straight ahead as he spoke.

"The children have also received ten miraculous secrets. They say the secrets must remain a mystery until an appointed time which only they know. The secrets will then be released to the world, one at a time, through a priest who will read them from a parchment. He will not be able to read the parchment until he has fasted and prayed for seven days. The messages will then in turn be announced to the world three days before each event is to occur."

For the next two minutes, the room stood so profoundly silent that it might as well have been empty. They were spellbound, each pilgrim lost in his own private contemplation. The driver handed the card back to his assistant, who put it in his coat pocket. Tony noted their veiled but cryptic reactions and thought, *there's more to these guys than first meets the eye. Every one of them has a story.*

CHAPTER 4

THE MYSTERY

Thursday, 3:30pm

They sat in silence for several minutes, until Tony could take it no more.

"Wow!" he said. "It's one thing to read about it in a book. It's quite another to be here. That gave me goosebumps. And as I'm sure you all know, Mirjana, herself, is gonna be there tomorrow! Her first appearance in years." He paused to let it sink in. "And, I might add, the last two certifiable miracles that took place at Medjugorje, just happened to occur when? That's right! When Mirjana was present. I read that on the Medj-America web. I'm tellin' ya, if a miracle's gonna happen...it's gonna be tomorrow!"

Even as the words were leaving his mouth, the thought was reassuring to him. He just *knew* something special was going to happen.

"What is the Medj-America Web?" inquired Amir.

"It's a website," said Tony, "the official American website for all visions of the Virgin."

The Croat looked at Tony and shook his head.

"Not much is really sacred in your country, is it?"

As was his habit, Tony simply continued.

"It also pointed out the fact that the Virgin chose to preach her message of peace in a land that was just about to witness one of the bloodiest wars the world had ever seen."

"Yes, I doubt that particular irony has eluded any of us," said the professor.

"It also listed several incredible phenomenon that have happened since the first vision, and not just in Medjugorje! A statue of Our Lady of Medjugorje cried tears of blood after being brought from Medjugorje to Italy!"

The man in the suit stood up dramatically holding a newspaper in front of him.

"It says here an American Director cried tears of blood in Medjugorje, after being stabbed by fellow passengers at a rest stop in Herzegovina. The passengers claimed: he just would not shut up!"

"The statue was declared "supernatural" by a panel of Italian theological experts, who spent nearly two years studying it!"

"Two years?" cried the Croat.

"A union job, no doubt," joked the professor. "I remember that! Shortly after the 'Madonina,' as they called the statue, began crying tears of blood, dozens of such bleeding statues began appearing all over Italy!"

Tony sensed the mood changing. They were lightening up. That was good. If they opened up, he'd get more material.

"When I was doing my research, it said that the Virgin used to appear to the kids daily, but after a while she told them she'd only appear to each of them on their birthdays and on the birthday of her son, December 25th."

"Doesn't *that* tell you something?" said the man in the suit.

"Should it?" asked Tony.

"You don't find it…interesting that she should call December 25th the day of her son's birth?" the man asked with a chuckle.

"Why do you find her appearing on Christmas so strange?" he asked.

"Oh, please!" laughed the professor.

"Why? The Virgin doesn't remember what day she gave birth to your Savior?" snarled the man in the suit.

The remark set off the driver's assistant who slammed his fist on the table and leapt up.

"Hey! Watch your mouth!" he shouted, as loud as he could manage through his voice buzzer. The sound actually had the unintended effect of making the white-haired guy laugh out loud. The assistant flared his nostril and looked as if he'd kill the man in the suit, when his cell phone rang. He let it ring several times before answering it. The look on his face changed and he immediately forgot his anger. He put on his coat as he spoke and headed back outside into the rain.

"Surely, everyone knows the December 25th date was a creation of calendar makers long ago," said the professor.

"Surely. Everybody but me, apparently," said Tony.

"No one knows the actual date," said Amir.

The Croat gave them all a look as though they were insane.

"What the hell are you talking about? Of course they do."

"No date is given anywhere in the Bible."

"Then why do we celebrate it on December 25th?"

"The birth of the Christ was first celebrated on December 25th in the 4th century, under the Roman Emperor Constantine, the first Christian Roman Emperor."

"How come?" asked Tony.

"Winter Solstice and the Roman midwinter festival took place in December. To the pagans, the end of winter and arrival of spring was something to celebrate."

"*Now,*" said the man in the suit, "don't you find it a little bit curious that the Virgin herself should refer to December 25th as her son's birthday? Or is it more likely that superstitious, fanatical children should make the claim?"

"Sorry, still not getting it," said Tony. "Why spring is so special?"

"Hello? So they could eat? Rebirth? Crops, food?" said Amir.

"Wait a minute, now you're saying Christmas is a pagan holiday?" asked the Croat.

"The truth hurts!" said the man in the suit with a laugh.

"Not so fast, my orthodox friend, your calendar is a mess too!" the professor said.

"Yeah, yeah, I know, we celebrate on the feast of Epiphany, when the Wise Men visited Christ."

"Actually, no. A common mistake. When the switch from Julian calendar to the Gregorian was made, ten days were lost. Since Orthodox Churches still use the Julian calendar, they celebrate Christmas on January 7th."

"That's not the way we learned it in Belgrade," he said.

"Ha!" cried out Amir as he put his hand out in front of the Croat. "Pay up, dude!"

The Croat took a bill from his wallet and gave it to him.

"Told you he was a Serb! Even 500 years ago Serbs were living in the past!"

Amir put the bill in his wallet and his wallet in his pants. Then he turned to the professor.

"Tell me, at what school do you teach?"

"Hmm?" said the professor, caught off guard. "Oh, in Ljubljana."

"Yes, but at which school?"

"Um, the National University."

Amir was confused but he did not pursue the matter further. To his knowledge, and it was a substantial amount of knowledge, there was no National University in Ljubljana. Something didn't add up.

"You see!" said Tony. "This is much more like it! We've much more in common than…"

"Oh, shut up! Will you?" growled the Serb.

Another tense silence descended. Amir wanted to know more about the professor but didn't want to appear too eager. So he changed the subject.

"So tell me, where was this orphanage you worked in, Tony?" he asked.

"In a town called Tuzla. But, let me tell you about the movie first…"

"Wait, what was the name of the orphanage?"

Tony had to think for a moment.

"Something like the Tuzla Home for Wayward children with no parents, something long like that."

"The Tuzla Home for Children without Parental Care," said Amir, mechanically.

"That's it! You know it?"

"I should, I lived there for almost eight years."

Now a different kind of silence hovered.

"To be honest," said Tony in a voice just above a whisper, "It's really a lot nicer than I thought it'd be."

Amir laughed out loud, "It's practically the Ritz Hotel!"

"What I mean is…"

"He knows what you mean," interrupted the Croat, "Why don't you give it a rest?"

"No, no. *Oprosti*," said Amir. "Go on. I want to hear more about your trip."

"You just said: "*Oprosti*?" said Tony with a big grin. "I know that one! That means: I'm sorry! Right? Huh? Huh? Chalk one up for the American?"

It's somehow fitting that you know that one," laughed the professor. "Have to use it often?"

"No. It was the title of a really cool tune I heard."

"By Gibonni!" interjected the Croat.

"Yes! You know it?"

"Everybody knows it. It was big hit a few years ago."

Tony stood up and started to swagger a bit.

"Well, let me tell you a little story about that song—"

"Wait, wait, wait, one story at a time!" said the professor.

"Yes, yes," agreed Amir. "You were telling us about your trip?"

"Right. Okay, so, we left New York and hopped a plane to Amsterdam. There we hopped another plane to *Zagreb*."

"*Za*-greb," interrupted the Croat.

"What?"

"It's pronounced *Za*-greb, not Za-*greb*. Look, rule of thumb, always accent on first syllable, ok?"

"Oh, cool! And thank you! OK, so anyway, we get to *Za*-greb and hop in cars and drive for like a day till we get to *Tuz*-la." He annunciated in the Croat's direction. "Anyway, we stay at this dilapidated hotel called, the um, hang on!" He opens up his backpack and pulls out a towel with a hotel name on it. "Here we go… the Hotel Bristol."

"You stole a towel from the hotel?" said Amir with visible disgust.

"OK, stop. Everybody does it. They practically expect it," said Tony.

"Don't you have any idea how poor those people are?"

"I sure do, the place was a dump!"

"Three years of shelling will do that," said Amir standing and walking to the window.

Tony thought this was total bullshit. For Chrissakes, it's a friggin' towel! He was annoyed that the Muslim kid was making a big deal of it. He didn't believe the indignation was genuine for even a second; just more Bosnian woe-is-me grandstanding. But he couldn't afford any trouble just when he'd gotten them talking, so he decided to eat another spoonful of shit.

"I left a very healthy tip," he said sympathetically. "C'mon! It's just a towel."

"How quintessentially American of you," stated the professor.

"Meaning?"

"Meaning, a tip erased all sins. Meaning this time: c'mon, it's just a towel. In 1944, it was: c'mon, they're just Jews. In Bosnia it was: c'mon, they're just Muslims."

Tony was pissed and he couldn't hold it back now.

"This is some kind of sport to you, right? You guys sit around all day, thinking up bigger and better ways to put down Americans. Talk about an inferiority complex!"

"Did your shrink teach you about that?" said the Serb.

"You know, you're all such experts at knocking America. But let me ask you this: if we suck so much, how come all I've seen since I got here is American culture, American clothes, American music?" He moved over to the Croat and grabbed his pack of Marlboro from the table. "American cigarettes? If we're so friggin awful, why are you all trying so desperately to be like us? Huh? Tell me that!"

He threw the cigarettes back to the Croat and walked over and sat at the counter.

"We're not trying to be like you," said the Croat. "We are envious of the things you have; not what or who you are."

"Wrong! What you perceive us to be!"

"Well, you've done precious little to change that perception, I'm afraid," said the professor.

By now, Tony was spoiling for a fight.

"Oh really? How? You gonna judge me because I mis-pronounced a few words? Ya know, it wouldn't kill you guys to throw a vowel or two into your words once in a while." He walked from table to table making certain no one missed out on his oration. "Or is it because I don't know as much about the culture as *you* deem appropriate? Ya know what? I didn't have to come here. I could just as easily have made a documentary about Hurricane Katrina victims or any number of other things, but I didn't. I came here because I heard about those kids in the orphanage and I hoped that maybe, just maybe, my film could shine a little light on this godforsaken dump of a country, and help the kids a little, OK? And if you have a problem with that, tough shit! It's your problem, not mine!"

After a prolonged silence, Amir was the first to speak.

"For the first time today, I agree with the American."

With a look of complete disbelief, Tony said, "Thank you. And it's Tony."

"What's Tony?"

"My name, it's Tony."

"Like Tony Kukoc?" said the Croat.

Amir just laughed.

"He didn't know *No Man's Land*, and you expect him to know Kukoc?"

"Hey, I never saw "No Man's Land" either! I didn't need any movie to tell me what happened in the war! But everybody knows Tony Kukoc! He's the greatest basketball player ever to come out of this country!"

"Excuse me?" said the Serb. "What about Vlade Divac?"

"I said *this* country."

"Actually, you are both wrong," said Amir. "Divac is a Serb, Kukoc is Croatian, but we are presently in Herzegovina."

Tony instinctively grabbed his iPad and started writing down every word. He was grateful that he'd kept the iPad in his backpack and not his suitcase.

"This is all great! What was the second fella's name?"

"Vlade Divac?" asked the Serb, dripping with sarcasm. "He played for a small, little known team in America called the Los Angeles Lakers. With Magic Johnson and Kareem Abdul Jabbar. Perhaps you have heard of them?"

"Heard of them? Shit, I did blow with them so many times, anyway, the point is…"

"The point is, you got to Tuzla," interrupted the professor impatiently.

Tony gave him dirty look, then a fake smile and continued.

"Oh yeah, Tuzla. Anyway, we get to Tuzla and they take us to the department of health for check-ups; as if we are going to give them something! So, we get a clean bill of health and it's off to the orphanage."

Amir was getting visibly annoyed with Tony's cavalier attitude toward the details.

"Again," he said, "we call it a home, not an orphanage."

"Look, no disrespect. By the way, what's your name again?"

"Amir."

"Look Amir, seriously, orphans live there, on my planet, that makes it an orphanage. It's just a fancy name for…"

"It is not a fancy name for anything!" raged the Bosnian. "The children who live there are without families for many different reasons. Some *are* orphans, but some are runaways, some abused, some abandoned."

"And which were you?" quipped the Serb.

"I wasn't speaking to you," said Amir.

Tony realized he was getting a bit too carried away and decided once again to take the volume and the pressure down a notch or two. He walked over to Amir and extended his hand.

"Sorry. No harm intended."

After a moment's introspection, Amir shook his hand.

"No, no harm at all!" laughed the Serb. "Just garden variety arrogance, that somehow it's just not important enough to get the details correct."

The beat-on-the-American bullshit was getting old and Tony wasn't sure how much more he could take.

"Hey! What the hell is wrong with all of you? There's no need to be nasty all the goddamn time, OK? Look, I haven't insulted any of you."

"Well, at least not intentionally," said the Serb as he blew a smoke ring toward Tony. Tony was tempted to hit him. He knew the others would support him but instead he just walked away.

"Tony! Go on, please," said Amir.

Tony cracked his knuckles and stretched.

"So, as I started to say, I'm supposed to spend a week in Tuzla, but the kids there really weren't very talkative. It would have taken more time than I had to break through to them so I decided to go to Split."

"You went to Split?" asked the Croat.

"Actually. I went to Sarajevo next. I needed to see it."

"Why Sarajevo?" asked the Croat again.

"Well, for obvious reasons, that's where most of the real hot action took place."

"What an asshole," said the Croat standing up and walking over to sit at the bar.

"For Chrissake, what now?" asked Tony, exasperated. "What did I say this time?"

"Real action took place everywhere, you fucking idiot. Right where we sit. The whole country was a war zone!"

"Of course, I know that, but I mean, c'mon guys! You know what I meant. The real hot stuff!"

"Forget it! He doesn't get it," said Amir to the Croat.

"No! I do get it. But can you guys just hold your indignation till the end of my story? Listen first, then judge. Okay? The screenplay, for the movie I'm making, takes place in a town called Bealina, where—"

"Bjeljina! Byell–yina," corrected the Serb.

"Thanks. So, my driver tells me that a horrible massacre took place there during the war. My story takes place in just that sort of village. An American tourist is taking a bus thru the beautiful countryside when the bus breaks down. The bus driver tells him it's going to be morning before they can get going again."

"This is starting to sound familiar!" joked the Croat.

Tony sensed the mood lightening again so he continued.

"So, the American wanders into the town to find a place to spend the night. As he does, he comes upon a wedding! Seeing how he's stranded, one of the locals ask him to join the party. They teach him some of the local dances and the local songs, and everything is going great until....BOOM! Shelling starts, tanks roll in, and just like the pogrom scene in "Fiddler on the Roof," the Serbs come in... and they massacre the whole wedding party! But!"

He paused for dramatic effect.

"The American saves the bride from the attack and the two of them escape. At first they hate each other but need to stick together to survive. They start an epic journey from Bealina to Sarajevo to Split where they hop a boat to freedom in Italy!"

He paused and caught his breath.

"Along the way... they learn the value of tolerance and forgiveness. They may even fall in love—I haven't decided yet if that's too far-fetched, but it would help the marketability of the script."

He looked at their silent faces, which betrayed no emotion.

"So? Whaddaya think?"

The silence continued for a long awkward moment until finally the professor spoke.

"What do I think? I think you did a little too much "blow" with Magic Johnson."

Tony rolled his eyes, "No, seriously. As a historian, what do you think? Stick to the facts. Did you notice any glaring inaccuracies?"

"I, I'm not even sure where to begin, but, I'm pretty sure that there were no tourist buses running in Bosnia during the war."

Like a light bulb, it dawned on Tony. Crap. That was an obvious one. How the heck didn't he think of it?

"See?" he said. "That makes sense. I didn't think of it. Thank you."

He turned to Amir.

"And what about you?"

"I'm not clear on exactly how they learned these valuable lessons about tolerance and forgiveness?"

"OK. Point taken. I need to expand on that. Remember, it's still just a really rough draft and I need to polish it, but this is all good."

He moved on to the Croat.

"And you? By the way, I never got you name."

The Croat stared at Tony in complete astonishment.

"Did you really just compare our war to *Fiddler on the fucking Roof?*"

"Of course he did," said the Serb with a laugh. "It's all just entertainment to him! No one dies or loses limbs fighting in America! The Home for Children in Tuzla? Just another diversion! They come, take pictures with the children to show their friends, and feel good about themselves. Then they go home to their comfortable homes in suburbia, and never come back! The children are accessories! Cocktail conversation!"

"That's fine coming from you, since you put most of them there in the first place!" said Amir.

"I put no one anywhere and I'm not going to waste my breath—"

"C'mon guys! Cool it!" said Tony. "We're finally making some progress here!"

"What progress? What is this, the United Nations?" said the Croat. "We're on a Goddamn bus ride!"

"And a very long one at that," said Tony. "And it'll only get longer if we're at each other's necks."

"Might I point out," said the Serb with his usual sarcasm,

"that if you hadn't stirred everyone up, we would have traveled to Medjugorje in perfect peace and quiet."

"Might I point out...I realize that. But as the bible says: blessed are the peacemakers! And I plan to try to make friends of all of you before we get there!"

A collective groan filled the room. The old man behind the counter smiled and began to chuckle to himself. He'd seen Americans like this one before and always wondered why they felt the need to tell everybody what to do. Then, as if reading his mind, the Serb spoke.

"Why is it so important to get involved? Why can't you just leave people alone?"

"Yes, like you left Bosnia alone from 93 to 95," said Amir.

Tony spun around to face Amir.

"Excuse me! I seem to recall, it was the U.S. that stepped in and stopped this thing and saved all your asses!"

"Yes, after half a million Muslims were slaughtered!"

"My family had no water or electricity for three months!" yelled the Croat.

"Three months? Are you kidding? In Sarajevo, we had no power for three years!"

The Serb stood up and motioned to the old man for more coffee.

"You both conveniently forget that the biggest genocide since the Holocaust was perpetrated against the Serbs by the Croats in the *Ustashe* Concentration camps! Nearly a million men, women, and children perished."

"That was a half century ago and the United Nations put the number at 70,000—not a million," interjected the professor.

"And the U.N. also put the number of Jews dead in the Holocaust at four million, but the Jews insist it was six million. Fifty years from now they will say ten million!"

"Holy Shit! You guys really can't agree on anything," said Tony. "I don't understand why there's so much vitriol in every conversation." He immediately regretted the choice of words; but hoped no one would understand them. He also realized the chance of these guys having a civil conversation was virtually nil. The almost congenital pessimism which he had been warned about by the travel agent hung thickly in the air. It seemed as though a long dark night had fallen upon these people and no one seemed to believe a new day could possibly dawn. Any glimmer of hope, any promise of a better future, was rapidly drowning in a sea of apathy.

Suddenly, he had an idea. He got up and opened up his backpack.

"Hold on just one minute. I've got an idea."

He dug through the backpack for something.

"I know it's here somewhere....yes! Okay, here, we go!"

He pulled out a small rather thin paperback book; more of a pamphlet, really.

"Ready? Okay, here goes: Everything You Ever Wanted to Know about the Virgin Mary But Were Afraid to Ask," he paused again for dramatic effect, "as told by the Blessed Virgin herself to the children of Medjugorje!"

The now familiar sound of stunned silence came over the room once more. It was broken by the old man, who started to laugh to himself as he came shuffling out from behind the counter.

"I need to go upstairs and change the towels. If you need anything, ring bell on counter. My daughter Marija is in kitchen. She will come."

He looked at Tony and started to laugh again, and he continued to laugh as he went up the stairs next to the bar, shaking his head.

Tony suddenly had a sinking feeling in the pit of his stomach.

CHAPTER 5

THE GAME

Thursday, 4:30pm

"You're kidding right?" said the Croat with a smile.

And mimicking the voice of a young child, the Serb said, "Does this mean you are going to read to us?"

Tony ignored them.

"Better! Gonna play a little Virgin Mary trivial pursuit!"

The chorus of incredulous groans returned. Behind the counter, the door to the kitchen opened just a crack and someone peered through at them. The words 'Virgin Mary' had caused somebody's ears to perk up and take a look into the dining room to investigate.

"Well, my friend," said the professor, "I hardly think it's a fair game!"

"How come?"

"Obviously because we're not all Christians."

"That doesn't mean anything. I'm a Presbyterian and I don't know shit about religion," said Tony.

"Perhaps you haven't noticed yet," said Amir, "but, we take our religion a bit more seriously around here."

"Yeah," said the Croat. "We fight wars over it."

"You mean you *lose* wars over it," said the Serb.

The Croat bull-rushed the Serb and knocked him to the ground, wildly punching at him. The two wrestled on the ground as the others tried to break them apart. After a minute, they separated them. The Serb got up and dusted off his clothes, while the Croat was still being held back by Tony and Amir.

"Fucking Chetnik pig!" he yelled and spat at him.

"He's not worth it," said Amir, trying to calm the Croat down.

"I'll kill you!"

"Yes, yes, that's the spirit," said the Serb resetting his watch. "You call me a pig but you are always the first with an insult or to throw a punch."

"Settle down, we'll be leaving soon and you'll never have to see each other again," said the professor, leading the Croat to a neutral corner of the restaurant.

Just at that moment, the driver's assistant came back inside from the rain and rushed over to the driver. The voice device buzzed a few words in Bosnian. The driver did not look at all pleased by the news. The assistant then went and took a stool at the bar.

"Nescafe!" he buzzed. It made Tony laugh but he quickly caught himself. The last thing he needed was them thinking he had made fun of a man with a handicap.

The Serb stood up and drained his coffee cup.

"Finally! Can we go now? We've been here over an hour already!"

The bus driver stood up and put one foot up on the chair to tie his shoe laces.

"Not just yet, I am afraid," he said.

"Why not?" asked the professor.

"The road is flooded. Another bus a mile ahead slid into a tree and turned over and is blocking the road. So we have to wait here until it's moved."

"Jesus friggin' Christ!" said Tony. Immediately, the driver's assistant got in his face.

"Hey! Do not blaspheme!" he buzzed. Tony bit his lip not to laugh and he nodded and piously made the sign of the cross to him. The assistant gave him a look of disgust and moved on. The driver sat back down, pulled out the small transistor radio and put it on.

"Any idea how long?" asked the Croat.

"Not too long. Maybe an hour?"

"But it's already been an hour You said we'd only be here twenty minutes!"

As the chorus of frustration filled the air again, the pilgrims all sat back down at the tables.

The Serb sat alone at the bar.

Tony pulled one of the bar stools over to the table that Amir and the Croat were sitting at and began to page thru his trivial pursuit book. He looked around and loudly cleared his throat.

"OK...I'll go first."

Silence.

"With or without you guys, I don't care."

He paged through the book.

"But, if you do know an answer, jump right in."

They continued to ignore him.

"OK, first question. Ready? On what date did the Virgin first—"

Almost unconsciously all of them replied together with one bored voice.

"June 24, 1981."

Tony was impressed.

"Hmm, guess I have to make the questions a little harder. OK, how about this one: to how many children did the Virgin appear..."

"Two," they all answered together again.

"I guess you guys really were paying attention to the driver's lecture."

The plan was slowly beginning to work. Give them something in common. He searched the book for another question.

"OK, what were the two girls..."

"Ivanka and Mirjana"

"Last names?" asked Tony with a twinkle

"Ivankovic and Dragicevic," said the bus driver.

He was the last person Tony expected to join the game.

"Correct!" he said, as the others grumbled. "OK, on the next day..."

"Four!" blurted out the Croatian.

"Wait! Um...forgive me...your name again?"

"Ivo," said the Croat.

"Okay, Ivo, you gotta wait till I finish the question. OK, on the next day, the girls returned with four friends, their names were?"

"That's a tough one," said the professor scratching his chin.

Meanwhile, from the doorway to the kitchen, the old man's

daughter, Marija was watching in silence, dying to join the game. She'd answered each of the questions silently to herself, but she was getting ready to burst. She was just about to call out the answers from behind the door when the bus driver again stole her thunder.

"Vicka Ivankovic, Ivan Dragicevic, Maria Pavlovic, Jakov Colo."

The whole group protested, "Not fair! He's reading the card! He knows these by heart!"

"Okay, okay. I'll mix it up a bit," said Tony. "Just give me a minute. Okay, I got it! No way! The driver has these memorized. Ready?"

"Yeah, yeah, let's go!" said Ivo, impatiently.

"Okay, the following are excerpts from interviews with Mirjana and Ivana regarding the physical appearance of the Virgin!"

"Oooooh, cool! Interesting!"

"First question: how tall is the Madonna?"

"How tall?" repeated the professor.

"Yes, how tall?" said Tony. As the pilgrims pondered the question, he started to hum the theme song from *Jeopardy!* After a few seconds with no replies coming, he made a buzzer sound.

"I'm sorry, time's up! The answer is 165cm or 5 feet, 5 inches tall."

Uniformly surprised faces stared back at him.

"Wow, I always imagined her taller," said Ivo.

"Okay next! Is she "slender," slim or…"

"Slim, slim," they all called out.

"Correct! Okay but how much does she weigh?"

"50 kilos!" said Amir.

"Are you crazy? No! Much less, like 43 or 44," said Ivo.

Tony once again hummed the *Jeopardy!* theme, then made the buzzer sound.

"Sorry, time's up! The answer is: about 60 kilograms or 132 pounds."

"Seems God likes them with a bit of meat on their bones," said the Serb.

"Yeah that would definitely make her a little chubby," said Ivo.

"You know, I never considered that before," said the Serb. "I wonder why there are no visions of the Virgin from the time Christ was actually crucified?"

"What do you mean?" asked the Croat.

"I mean, the Virgin is always described as young and beautiful."

"So?"

"Well by the time her son died, she had to be over fifty years old. Chances are she had a hard life. She must have had gray hair and wrinkled skin. Probably missing a tooth or two also. Why don't the artists or the vision-seers ever see her in her ripe old age? Why is she always young and beautiful? It is almost as though Hollywood was casting for the Virgin! Mr. Director, who would you cast as the perfect Virgin Mary?"

Tony didn't want to go down this road but as he looked around he saw everyone's imaginations were already at work.

"Okay. Let me think for a minute." As he thought, he glanced around and every set of eyes was wistfully squinting in deep thought. This might turn out alright after all, he thought.

"I've got it! Ready?" He paused to insure dramatic effect. "Salma Hayek!"

Several heads nodded in agreement, others shook in complete disdain.

"No way!" said the Croat. "I say Kiera Knightly!"

More nods and some broad smiles.

"How about Madonna?" said the Serb. "She already has the name."

They all laughed.

"Now *that's* what I call blasphemy!" said Tony.

The mood was substantially lighter and Tony didn't want to push his luck so he decided to continue with the game.

"Okay, keeping with theme, this is a good one. Ready? How old is she?"

"I know! She's two thousand and... kidding! Just kidding!" said the professor, although nobody really laughed.

"I believe the Bible said she was eighteen?" said Amir.

"Ding! Ding! Ding! That is exactly right!" said Tony.

Ivo high-fived Amir and Tony saw that for the first time, all of the pilgrims were actually smiling! Now he just had to keep it going.

"It seems, once again, our Muslim knows more about the Virgin than our Christians! Shame, shame!" said the professor with a laugh designed to zing his comrades. Suddenly, not everyone was laughing. The Serb was annoyed at the barb.

"And where exactly do you stand in this, then?" he asked.

The professor regarded the question and the questioner for a moment.

"I'm not sure I understand," he said.

"Yes, you do," said the Serb. "Before, you said: 'Oye ve!' Then you complained that 'the Christians' had an unfair advantage, now it's the 'Muslim and the Christians.' Well, you don't look Buddhist to me so I'm going to guess you lied. You are a Jew."

"What is it to you, my friend?" asked the professor gently.

"I'm not your friend."

"No, I don't imagine you are. In fact, I'd say you are friendless in this crowd. So, I'd tread carefully, *my friend*."

Tony was pissed. All the good will had just gone out the window. "Come on guys, tone it and play the game."

"Why?" demanded the Serb. "Must we be friends to play this silly game? What do you say—*my friend?*"

"I say," said Tony searching for the right words to restore the peace, "what color were the Virgin's eyes?"

"That's easy. Blue!" said Ivo.

"Ah, but she was from the Middle East, remember? How many blue eyed Arabs and Jews do you know?" asked the professor.

"I've never met an Arab or a Jew but I've seen plenty of paintings and the Virgin's eyes are always blue!"

The Serb laughed.

"Never met an Arab or a Jew? Are you blind? They are on either side of you!"

Tony ignored the remark and quickly continued.

"Correct! They are blue. And on what is she standing?"

"If you mean to suggest that I am the Arab in that equation then you are even more ignorant than I'd already imagined," said Amir.

"Guys, on what is she standing?"

"Obviously on a scale! So they could know her weight!" said Ivo laughing loudly at his own joke.

"She is standing on a cloud," said the professor.

"Correct."

"How'd you know that?" asked Ivo.

"Same as you, paintings!"

Tony felt some momentum again.

"Now, let's talk a bit about her personal appearance. The Madonna's nose, what is it like: sharp or…"

"Well," said the Serb, "she was a Jew, so it stands to reason the nose was hooked with a bump on it. Much like yours, my friend."

"I must say that until this moment I found the American the most annoying and difficult to tolerate in this little group, but you…"

"Just ignore him," said Ivo. "He's an asshole!"

"You're the asshole!" bellowed the Serb.

"Please!" yelled the professor over the clamor. "Can we at least try to act like human beings for a moment?" They all shut up. "Now, I may be wrong but I believe I speak for everyone here when I say: *you're* the asshole!"

Tony couldn't believe his eyes. In seconds, they were all screaming at one another at the top of their lungs again. He was engulfed in yet another cacophony of Croatian, Bosnian, and Serbian. He stood on a chair and put two fingers in his mouth and whistled a disturbingly loud and shrill whistle, which immediately stopped the arguing. It also had another effect; it brought a beautiful brown eyed, honey haired young woman out of the kitchen to investigate. She was ravishingly beautiful in a rough kind of way. She had large, wide-set, somewhat protruding eyes with lush long eyelashes. There were tired lines under her eyes that made her look older than she probably was. Her beauty was a youthful one, and sadly, that would soon pass.

Tony looked back at the crowd, now staring at him.

"If your little battle of wits is done, Uncle Tony needs a pit stop; try not to kill each other while I'm gone."

But nobody was listening to him. Every eye was on the girl behind the counter. She seemed completely out of place out here in the middle of nowhere. Tony smiled and nodded at her as he went to the restroom.

The professor walked over to the driver.

"Please! Please, tell me we can go and leave him here!"

"All in favor?" said the Serb.

"Aye!"

The bus driver just yawned at them. "Unfortunately, not possible. I want to keep my job. But, we should be on the road soon."

"We could have walked to Medjugorje by now!" said the frustrated professor.

"Good luck," said the driver. "These woods are not safe. They are full of bad spirits. Nobody travels these roads alone."

"Bad spirits?" said the professor.

"Demons," said the driver. "They say the devil lurks in these woods."

"Of course they do," said the professor as he wandered over to the window and watched the rain pour down outside. It had gotten much heavier and he was nervous that the temporary delay might not be so temporary. He had little faith in anything anymore.

The Men's room smelled of cigarettes, sweat, and cheap pine scented disinfectant. After he'd relieved himself, Tony washed his face and hands. There were no towels to dry his hands and he chuckled to himself, *typical.*

He looked at his reflection in the mirror and was surprised at how tired he looked. His eyes had deep dark circles beneath them; circles that he knew would probably never go away. People always told him that he looked just like his father, but he could never see it. He could, however, see faint traces of his mother's face in his own eyes and cheek bones. Maybe he saw it because he wanted to see it. People had also accused him of doing that—especially his wife. This trip was supposed to change all of that. So far it had been only mildly successful, but there was still time. He needed to stop preaching to these guys, but it wasn't easy! He felt compelled to defend America and defend himself over and over again. He used to spend most of his time putting down his country and its government which he perceived as an oligarchy in the making, squeezing the blood out of the middle class, or what was left of it. He firmly believed that the United States operated on the presumption that just because something worked for, or was good for, the U.S., it must therefore work for and be good for the entire world. The problem with this logic was simple: *The U.S. didn't even have the first clue what was good for itself. If it did, we'd never be in the mess we're in.*

But here, for some reason, he couldn't help defending and trying to explain every single political, cultural, and ideological aspect of America. Coupled with these inexplicable feelings were his conflicting sentiments about being back in Bosnia. During the months away from the country and its people, he tried hard but ultimately failed to fully comprehend the country's unnatural hold on him.

He threw water in his face and shook like a wet dog. He needed to resist the temptation to engage and just sit back and listen;

become part of the scenery. Observe. Take notes. Nothing more. Tony wasn't a liar by nature or a dishonest person, although he did have an overly healthy sense of hyperbole. He used to joke with Claire: "C'mon, honey! By now you really should know to take 10 percent off the top of whatever I tell you!"

In those days, he could talk for hours without pausing. Thoughts and sentences poured out of him like a mountain spring after a heavy rain. Everyone loved his stories—or so he thought. It was only after going fully on the wagon that he realized what a bore he was capable of being. A true storyteller, he never gave a second thought to the rigid boundaries of truth, and he was certain he'd be lying through his teeth before the night was over.

He looked down at his watch and thought about the decision he'd made that morning. It lingered in the back of his mind, both threat and promise. He had to pick up the pace but not appear impatient.

He tended to treat each of them the same, which was by design, but he also needed to be mindful of the fact that although they appeared identical to him in so many ways, they did not view themselves as such. There were many tiny distinctions between them, but the very distinctions that seemed insignificant to him were categorical contrasts to them—differences worth fighting for, even dying for.

CHAPTER 6

ALLIANCES

Thursday, 6:00pm

The professor looked out the window at the rain drops forming puddles in the parking lot, and he felt a slight tightness in his chest. *No more coffee or cigarettes. Yeah right, that wouldn't last long.* He was talking much more than he wanted to be and much more than he thought wise. That damned American had dragged him into the middle of a conversation that he couldn't resist. This was no way to keep a low profile. He decided that it would be wisest to say as little as possible until they reached Medjugorje.

Amir got up from the table and casually strolled over to join the professor by the window. He tried to look nonchalant but it wasn't working.

"The rain is worse," he said.

"I hate driving the mountain roads in the rain," replied the professor.

"Don't worry, these drivers are like *koze*, billy goats, they know the roads like the back of their hands."

He wanted to ask a question but didn't quite know how to phrase it. If he chose poor words, he sensed that the professor, who clearly prized his privacy, might close up altogether. Amir decided to make a game of it.

"So, tell me, why does a Slovenian History Professor travel to America so often?"

The professor gave Amir a long stare. *So much for saying as little as possible*, he thought.

"You ask a lot of questions."

"I'm a student, that's what I do. I'm currently studying in Sarajevo, but when I graduate, I hope to work in America. Perhaps you can give me some pointers…some advice… *a job?*"

The professor gave him an even longer once over. He appeared satisfied with what he saw.

"Okay, I'll see what I can do. Do you have a card or a number?"

"Yes, yes. Both!" said Amir. "And I'll be graduating next spring and looking for work. Slovenia isn't that far."

"You from Sarajevo originally?"

"No, Srebrenica. Then Zvornik. Then Tuzla. Now Sarajevo."

"You certainly get around," said the professor, beating around the bush before he asked the real question.

"Srebrenica, huh? I see. And how old are you now?"

"I was there, when it happened, if that's what you're getting at."

The professor looked at Amir and in his mind he did the math. The kid had to have been in his early teens when it happened.

"There are few left to tell the tale."

"I don't want to talk about it."

"I understand." He thought for a moment about what it must have been like, to be a child and witness a massacre. How do you even get up each day? "I understand. But, if you, you know…feel the need to…unburden yourself…"

"I carry no burden. I've moved on," said Amir. The professor patted him on the shoulder and sighed.

"You will, my friend. You will."

The professor felt torn. His desire to provide council and to help was stronger than his desire to remain inconspicuous. After standing in silence for a minute, he pulled Amir close and whispered to him.

"Alright, my brave friend, here's my first piece of advice. You seem to have become friendly with the Croatian."

"Ivo? Yes. He's a truck driver, like my father was. A simple fellow, but nice."

"That's all well and good, but heed my words carefully: he and the Serb will eventually mend fences and when they do…"

"Are you crazy? They practically killed each other!"

The professor looked into the young student's eyes and saw inexperience and naivety. He was envious of the younger man and that envy made him wistful.

"Hear me and learn. There is an old Bosnian expression: In the end, CROSSES ALWAYS TAKE CARE OF CROSSES. Never forget that."

CHAPTER 7
ЦХАПТЕР 7

MARIJA
МАРИЈА

Thursday, 6:15pm

Tony emerged from the bathroom with clean hands and fresh determination.

"Okay, everybody ready for round two?" he said.

"No!" they all answered.

"Whoa, how do you really feel?"

He decided it was best to let them relax for a while—a short while. If even a simple parlor game could set them off at any minute, maybe he should let sleeping dogs lie for a while. But he knew he could not let them sleep for long, because his time here was limited and he still needed a lot more information. When they got indignant, they let the information flow, and that was productive. But that indignation had a nasty habit of spiraling out of control and getting physical. He needed to recalibrate for a minute.

He glanced over at the counter and noticed the girl wiping it down with a towel. She really was quite beautiful in a natural, unpolished kind of way. He glanced at her hands as she worked and noticed they were exceedingly rough-looking. Clearly, she was no stranger to hard work, and accordingly, a lot of harsh cleaning products. She'd probably been busting her ass in this dump every day of her young life.

He sat at the counter and wondered if she might be a good source of info. She was probably only eighteen or so, and that would have made her just a very small child during the war, but she would have seen it all. Tony thought he could see it in her eyes, just as he had seen it in the eyes of the children in Tuzla. The kids had the brightest eyes he'd ever seen, bespeaking a joy he hadn't know since he himself was a child—and maybe not even then. But as they say, the brightest of eyes often conceal the darkest of secrets, and these eyes had surely seen a lot, far more than they should have been asked to see.

Tony noticed a yellowing old sign in a frame behind the counter that said in several languages, including English: "NO CREDIT." It made him smile. It looked like a throwback to the cold war era— probably was.

During the cold war, he had learned, all of the bars in Eastern Europe insisted upon hard currency. That was an easy and effective way to keep out all the undesirables (including the communists who famously never had any money to spend!)

The girl behind the counter had looked away each time their eyes had met. Clearly she was a bit shy, but Tony was determined to make contact. He smiled at her and she nervously smiled at him. She had a great smile. Some orthodontia as a child might have helped, but she had a wonderful earthy quality about her.

"I made some fresh cookies, would you like one?" she asked. Her English was far more heavily accented than the others but Tony was thrilled that she spoke it at all; that would make it a lot easier and hopefully, more productive.

"Ah! Yes! Thank you. What are they?"

She fidgeted nervously, "they are cookies."

"Yes, of course they are," he said with a laugh as he took one from the plate.

"So…are you really a Hollywood movie director?" she asked trying hard to conceal her excitement.

"I sure am."

"Wow. Cool." She smiled and self-consciously tucked her long hair behind her ears, showing more of her lovely Slavic features. She had large and very pronounced cheek and chin bones, the kind the camera tended to like.

"You have wonderful bone structure. I think you would look great on film."

She blushed.

"Really? I once had a photographer take my picture, to use in a tourist advertisement. I was never happy with it. It made me look old, I thought."

"Have you done anything else? Any other modeling, acting?"

"I was in holiday plays in school. The teacher told me I was a fine actress." She bit her bottom lip as she spoke.

"Really?" said Tony with a nod. "Have you done anything since then?"

"No, no. I have to work. It's just Papa and me and the days are long."

"I'm sure they are," he said in a voice tinged with sadness. Another time another place, she might have had a career. She wasn't a classic beauty but there was certainly something about her that was captivating. "That's a shame. Because you have a real earthy beauty to you, a certain honesty. I'll bet you would have been a wonderful actress."

She almost giggled at the compliment but caught herself when she saw her father coming down the stairs. The transformation was sudden and complete; it was back to business.

"Um...would you like anything else? Some more coffee?" she said with a forced yawn.

"Yes, please. Can you make it a decaf with skim and a smile, if it's not too much trouble," he said with a wink. She was lost.

"Please?" she asked.

"Decaf with skim milk."

Now she was nervous. Apparently her English didn't extend that far. Her father stepped behind the counter and with a grim expression took charge. He scolded her in Bosnian and she went back into the kitchen.

"Sorry, did I do something wrong? If I did, I..."

"What do you want?" asked the old man.

Tony tried again. "Decaf coffee with skim milk." The old man stared at him, not understanding the request. Ivo came over to the counter and looked through the magazines scattered there.

"Hey, Ivo. Gimme a hand here will ya?"

"What's the problem?"

"I'm trying to order a decaf coffee with fat free milk."

Ivo made a face, "Why?"

"*Why?*"

"Yes. Why?"

"Because that's what I drink."

"There is no such thing as decaf in this country."

"You're kidding."

"No. And there's no such thing as milk without fat and there's no such thing as coffee "to go." Shall I go on?"

Damn, he thought. He hated when he got caught as the "ugly American." He had guarded so hard against it.

"No, no! Just get me, just get me a coffee, any kind."

The old man continued to look at him, his confusion turning to anger.

"*Ma, kreten! Samo mu daj tursku!*" said Ivo, basically telling the old man in Croatian that Tony is some kind of "faggot" American who wants coffee with no caffeine and milk with no fat. Don't worry, just bring him Turkish coffee.

The Serb burst out laughing at Ivo's remarks. Across the room, Amir noticed the two of them laughing together and immediately thought of the professor's admonishment to him. He glanced over at the professor who smiled knowingly and nodded.

"Thanks, Ivo. I wasn't hitting on her or anything. In LA, when a waitress asks how I like my coffee I usually say: with a kiss."

"And that doesn't get you a slap in the face?" asked the Serb.

"Shit, no. Usually it gets me a phone number! Sometimes more."

Tony took his little cup of Turkish coffee and walked around Ivo and sat next to the Serb.

"Tell me something," he said softly, "I know you guys don't get along, but, what's the point of constantly being confrontational? I'm no expert but, I mean, you seem like a bright guy, a professional, and yet you don't even try to be civil. You are one rude dude, man."

"I won't answer you with the indignation that that question deserves because I know it will sound hopelessly clichéd to you. But, you could not possibly understand unless you've lived generations in our shoes."

"You do realize that the righteous indignation bit is getting really old really fast, right? But seriously, you guys are a young country! Even Yugoslavia, if I'm correct, was only around since WWII, right?"

"Countries are lines on a map to you. Yours is the young country. The Hapsburgs controlled the largest, richest empire since the Romans. Our race dates back to pre-Roman times, our disputes just as far. So please, don't waste my time trying to solve all of the Balkan's problems over coffee and cake. Americans think everything can be boiled down to a simple answer."

"Because," said Tony, "it usually can. If you want it to. But first, you have to want it to."

The Serb stood up and yelled, "Oh my God! That's it! Why has no one before thought of that? I will alert all the media!"

"Oh, shut up!" said Tony. "I was trying not to go along with the crowd against you but you're making it awfully hard."

"Oh, no! Dear, dear, what will I do? The American is trying to be my friend and I am making it hard for him!"

"Fine! Goodbye, asshole!"

Tony got up from the counter and walked to the window. Outside in the parking lot, huge puddles were forming. It was definitely getting worse and not better. Things were not progressing as he'd hoped and he was beginning to fear that he wouldn't be able to complete his mission. Suddenly there was someone at his side. It was Amir.

"Look, I don't want to talk about politics! Okay?" said the Bosnian.

"What's that supposed to mean?" snapped Tony.

"Nothing. But I mean it!"

"Hey," said Tony, "you walked over here, not me." He looked at the young Bosnian and thought that he was his best chance at a real ally. "But, to be honest, I was sorta hoping you might be interested in consulting on my film."

Amir regarded him with a suspicious eye. "Consulting?"

"Yeah, and something like an Associate Producer credit for your labors?"

"Really?"

"Absolutely, that is if you're interested?"

"Sure, I guess. What do I need to do?"

"Help me fill in some of the blanks. I've done tons of research about this country and the war and the ethnic conflict, but this is my first real 'boots on the ground' investigation."

"Okay, so?"

"So? Apparently all that work was for nothing. Seems I really don't have as much of a grasp on things here as I thought. You all laughed at my ideas but no one would say why. I wanna know why? Not simply: 'Our race dates back to Roman times. So please don't waste my time trying to solve all of the Balkans problems over coffee and cake.'" He said, imitating the Serb.

Amir laughed, "Hey, you do a pretty good Schwarzenegger!"

"Thanks. I was going to ask the Serb to help out too but I hate working with assholes and that guy is a grade-A A-hole!"

"He can't help it. It's part of his genetic code. But what he said is right."

"Then correct me! I'm not an idiot. I want to learn. You guys aren't exactly generous with your knowledge if you know what I'm sayin'. Help me out. Tell me what I'm missing."

After debating for a few seconds, Amir led him to a table and sat down.

"Okay, the basics," he said as if searching for the right words to use. "Within Bosnia, there live three separate religious groups: Muslims, Catholics, and Orthodox Christians. You already know that much. Now, the Muslims are known as Bosniaks, the Catholics are called Bosnian Croats, and the Orthodox are Bosnian Serbs. Got it?"

Tony slowly nodded, "Okay. Got it."

Ivo cleared his throat loudly, as if he did not agree.

"Whoa! Wait a minute!" he said.

"Relax, I'm not done!" said Amir. "Now, these are all just names the international community has given them, not what they actually call themselves. Croats think of themselves simply as Croats. The same with Serbs. Do you understand?"

"Sure, I see. Cool. Okay, so, let me get this straight: Catholics in Bosnia are called Bosnian Croats." Then he added in Ivo's direction: "By the international community. And Orthodox Christians in Bosnia are called Bosnian Serbs!"

"Correct."

Tony felt a moment of pride and communion with the group.

"OK, that's what you call them here, but what would you call a Bosnian in Serbia?"

"Dead," said the Serb without even looking up from his coffee.

They all glared him with fury in their eyes. And for a second, Tony thought that the Serb enjoyed it.

"Ignore him," said Amir, trying to keep his anger in check, "because what the idiot Serbs refuse to understand is that we've changed rulership literally hundreds of times, and hundreds of years ago the religion in a particular region was usually chosen simply as the lesser of two evils, or more often imposed by conquerors upon simple people who didn't want any trouble. In fact, our friend here probably doesn't even know that a hundred years ago the most powerful man in all Medjugorje was actually a Serb!"

"Really?" asked Tony.

"Yes. He owned the region's only vineyard and he became quite wealthy. He was beloved and beneficent and they were capable of living harmoniously."

"And tell our American friend what happened to him!" said the Serb. "Or don't you know? I'll tell you. He disappeared never to be heard from again, probably kidnapped. His house was ransacked and his vineyards burned to the ground by the local Croats and Muslims."

"He was run out of town because he began trying to convert the population to the Orthodox Church," said Amir. "He even petitioned to build an Orthodox Monastery in Medjugorje."

"And for that they killed him," said the Serb.

"Again, religion," said Tony. "It seems to me like religion is the culprit in all your disputes. What actual good has come of your religious faith in this region?"

"Religion is our moral compass," said the Croat. "It give our lives purpose."

"Why?" said Tony. "Let me ask you all a question. And I'll tell you right off that I'm not an overly religious guy. But tell me: is it better to 'love thy neighbor, and do unto him as you would like him to do unto you' because God or Allah *commands* it? Or is it better to 'love thy neighbor and do unto him as you would have him to unto you,' simply because it's the right thing to do? Because it is ethically and morally right. Why does religion have to get in the way of just doing the right thing?"

After a long moment of silence, Amir spoke. "It's complicated. And I don't have time to give you a complete history of the Balkans. You need to do the homework!

"No, no, no! That's fine. That's perfect! Exactly what I need, that kind of back ground. Just keep me inside the lines. Okay? So, you'll do it?"

"I don't know," said Amir, suddenly pissed off with the whole conversation.

Sensing he was losing him, Tony sat next to Amir and whispered.

"Look, the last thing I want is to try and tell you what to do. But, I was a student too once, not all that long ago. Okay, you're a student, but let's face it, you've got some mileage on you. You're not 18 or 20 anymore. The war set you back like what, ten years, maybe? Am I right?"

"So?"

"So, I'm willing to make you a full-fledged Associate Hollywood producer, just for answering a couple of questions. How's that gonna look on your resume?"

The arrow had pierced the bull's-eye. The raised eyebrows were always a dead giveaway. Tony thought of that great scene in "The Godfather" when Sonny said to Sollozzo: "Wait a minute, you mean to tell me that the Tattaglias are gonna..." And his father cut him off. But the damage was done. The Greek knew that Sonny was interested, just as Tony knew that Amir was interested.

"What do I need to do?

"I just need a cell number and an e-mail address to send stuff to you. Just take a red pen to it and send it back. It'll be great experience, you can make a few bucks and actually it should be a lot of fun."

"And that's it?"

"That's it."

"Cool."

Amir smiled, and the two shook hands.

"That wasn't so hard now was it?" Tony stood up and motioned for Amir to follow him. They walked as far from the rest of the group as they could. He put his arm over the Bosnian's shoulder and spoke in a voice just above a whisper.

"Okay, here's your first assignment. You see the professor over there?"

"Yes."

"There's something not right about him."

"What do you mean?"

"Think for a second: why exactly is a Jewish guy from Slovenia going to a Catholic shrine in a Muslim country?"

"Hmm. Good point. I hadn't even thought of that."

"Of course not. But as a director, I'm a bit of a student of human behavior. You two seem to be pretty chummy, see if you can get it out of him...discretely."

CHAPTER 8

THE MESSAGE

Thursday, 6:30pm

Tony walked to the counter, and tapped Ivo on the shoulder. Ivo promptly turned around and blew cigarette smoke in Tony's face.

"If smoking were an Olympic event," he coughed, "didn't you get the memo?"

"Memo?"

"Smoking kills!"

"Right. You do cocaine but you tell me not to smoke."

"Look, you think we could cut down on the smoking for a few minutes in here? I think I feel mesothelioma coming on."

"I never smoke in my whole life till I was about ten years old."

"Good for you. But, I'm tellin' ya; you're all gonna wind up like the Driver's assistant in a few years!"

Unseen behind him, the Serb blew smoke at him too.

"I cut back on my smoking, very much," said Ivo. "I almost never smoke more than one cigarette at a time."

Tony shook his head, "I think something got lost in translation there."

"Why doesn't anyone smoke in America anymore?"

The Serb let out a belly laugh.

"Someone must have told Americans that cigarettes contain fat!"

Ivo didn't get the joke and he was getting impatient.

"Did you want something?" he asked.

"Yeah, research," said Tony. "You're Catholic right?"

"So?"

"I want to know the Catholic point of view of Medjugorje?"

"Okay."

"First, can we possibly go and open up a window so I can breathe some fresh air?"

Ivo nodded and they walk to the window.

"You've got all this beautiful fresh mountain air," said Tony, "and you insist on polluting it with smoke." He opened the window and a massive wind gust nearly knocked him over. Fighting of a burst of rain, he re-shut it.

"You were saying?" said Ivo.

"Yeah," said Tony wiping his wet hands on his pants. "Tell me something Ivo; are you a religious man?"

"All Croats are religious," Ivo replied.

"Yeah, yeah, I know. But I mean, are *you* religious?"

Ivo looked at him, puzzled, "I just said, all Croats are religious."

"I heard you, but are you in particular religious?"

Ivo looked at him confused.

"Are you fucking retarded or something? If all Croats are religious and I am a Croat, I am religious. Okay?"

"Okay, okay! Never mind! Sheesh," said Tony. "I just wanted to see if you knew what the Catholic Church's stance is on the visions."

"Then why the fuck didn't you ask that?"

"I was getting to it."

"Okay, okay. Their opinion," said Ivo. "Well. It's simple. They have no opinion." And he walked away.

"That's it? They have no opinion?"

"That's it. Officially, they have no opinion. They do not recognize the visions or the miraculous cures."

"Why the hell not?"

"How the fuck should I know? Do I look like a priest?"

As if on cue, the professor cleared his throat.

"The church hasn't finished its investigation of the visions or the cures," he said. "These investigations take years. Often science will call something a miracle long before the church will; the church has much higher standards."

"They do?" asked Tony. "That makes no sense. Why?"

"Isn't it obvious? Science readily admits it is evolving," said the Professor. "Religion, on the other hand, is not evolving. It claims to always have been and always will be—therefore, it cannot afford to be wrong. Mistakes in religion lead to wars."

Tony got goose bumps. That was absolutely priceless. He ran to his iPad and started typing.

"That will make incredible dialogue! "Mistakes in religion lead to..." Hey, I'm sorry, I didn't get your name when you said it."

A hint of a smile crossed the professor's lips.

"Clever," he said. "I never said it."

"Oh, well then, what is it?"

The professor stared at Tony for a minute and smiled. "Bob. Call me Bob."

"Hmm, you don't look like a Bob, but, Okay, Bob. How'd you like to do some consulting? You clearly know more than me about, well about virtually everything. You could be a fact-checker or a researcher—anything you want. I think you'd be a real asset to the film. Whaddaya say?"

"I'll think about it," he said with a great big yawn.

"Awesome! You won't regret it, Bob!"

The Serb stood up and started to pace around impatiently. He walked over to the counter and whistled to the old man.

"It all means nothing. Science, religion, it's all bullshit," said the Serb.

"How can you say that?" asked Ivo.

"Have you a deck of cards?" he asked the old man.

The old man thought for a second.

"Yes," he said. "Upstairs in my room, I think. I go look." He took off his apron and placed it on a hook next to the door behind the counter, and then he went upstairs to look.

"How can I say that?" replied the Serb. "Because the facts support me. Every century, scientists think they have finally figured out the universe, and the next century rolls around and other scientists prove them wrong. The church stands on the sidelines maintaining its tired old mythology that any child can see is nonsense."

"Guys, haven't we had enough religion for one day?" said Tony.

"Are we boring you?" asked the Serb.

"Frankly? Yes. You are. Your arguments are utterly pointless and they solve nothing. And what's worse is that they inevitably degenerate to a disrespectful and insulting level. When it comes to religion, you have proven that all of you are incapable of having a simple, civil conversation."

For the first time all day, Tony had left them all speechless. He had met them on the field of intellectual battle and matched them wit for wit. He desperately hoped it would earn him their respect and not just more petty vindictiveness. He decided the time was right to lighten the mood again.

"Hey, we can always play more Virgin trial pursuit!" said Tony.

"No!" came the unified chorus.

Suddenly, Marija burst out from behind the counter.

"I would like to play," she said.

"What?"

"I said, I would like to play game about Blessed Virgin."

Tony smiled at her and nodded his head at all the others. "Ya see that? Ya see that? The faith of a child! Of course we can play, dear!"

"Oh, spare us," said the Serb.

"*Kako se zove, draga?*" asked Tony in a tender voice.

"*Kako se zove?*" laughed Amir and Tony winked at him.

"*Ja sam Marija*, I am named after the Blessed Virgin."

"Ah! So, you're Catholic then?"

"My Papa is Bosnian, but my mother, she is dead, she was Catholic."

"Is that common?"

"Yes," said the Serb, "it's very common for people to die here."

"Don't listen to him," said Ivo. "For centuries there was intermarriage in Croatia and in Herzegovina, very common."

"One might say the region was model of tolerance back then," said the professor.

"Oh, please!" said the Serb. "Fairytales! The very air you breathe here stinks of hatred!"

"Is that what that smell is? I thought it was Ivo," joked Tony, but it missed its mark.

"The Balkans have had nothing but bloodshed for a thousand years and always for the same old reasons," said the Serb.

"And now you'll tell us what those reasons are I'm sure," said Amir.

"You know very well what they are," raged the Serb. "Since 1398..."

"Here we go again!" said Tony, throwing his hands in the air.

"Please!" yelled Marija in a desperate voice. "I have only ten minute break! I want to play game!"

A general look of guilt spread across all of their faces.

"Well?" said Tony and they all nodded. "OK, Marija, sit down and we'll start."

She dashed over to grab a chair and sat right in the middle of them all.

"Now, I assume that since you are named after the Blessed Virgin, you must have a pretty good knowledge of the subject?"

"Please?" she asked.

"Never mind," said Tony, "Okay, first question: how many secrets has the Virgin given the children?"

"Ten."

"Okay, too easy. Next…"

"But," she interrupted, "only Mirjana, Ivanka, and Jakov have all ten secrets, Marija, Vicka, and Ivan have only nine secrets.

Tony looked at her like she had three heads.

"Really? Okay. How many *messages* has the Virgin given them?"

"Oh, too many to be counted."

"I don't suppose you could summarize them?"

"What?"

"Just kidding."

For just a minute, Tony considered that this girl could possibly be a font of information. He needed to probe a bit deeper.

"Okay," he said. "Why don't we drop the game and just ask Marija about…"

"Oh no! Please no! I like the game!" she said with an enormous smile.

"Okay. Okay, let's see." He leafed through the book looking for an especially tough one to really test her.

"Okay, here we go. Ready? Each vision since the very first has the same greeting. What is it?"

The entire group looked at Marija and Tony started humming the *Jeopardy!* song again.

"For God's sake! Must you constantly hum that annoying tune!" said the Serb.

"The Blessed Virgin begins every message since the very first, with two simple words: "Dear Children…"

The men were all silent with awe. Something was happening.

"Would you like to hear the entire first message?" asked Marija.

They all nodded. "Yes, yes, of course."

She cleared her throat and closed her eyes.

"One afternoon, Ivanka and Mirjana were walking home, passing a hill called Crnica, when suddenly Ivanka saw a bright silhouette of a woman. She said to Mirjana, 'It is the Gospa!'"

"The Gospa?" asked Tony.

"The name given to Our Lady! The Blessed Virgin Mary." Marija spread her hands wide, in a pose reminiscent of the Madonna as she continued.

"And the lady said to them: 'Dear children! Rejoice with me, convert in joy and give thanks to God for the gift of my presence among you. Pray that, in your hearts, God may be in the center of your life, little children, so that every creature may feel God's love. Be my extended hands reaching out to every creature, so they may draw closer to the God of love. I bless you with my motherly blessing. Thank you for having responded to my call.'" There was compete silence, except for the sound of the rain on the window pane. All eyes remained fixed on the girl.

"Wow," said Tony.

"Marija, how is it you know the message so well?"

"I know most of the messages. For some reason once I hear them, I cannot forget them. I think it is God's will."

"What do you mean: *once you hear them?*" asked Ivo. "You didn't read them? I mean from a book or…"

"I read them, but also, I have heard them from the children."

"What children?" asked the professor.

"From Ivanka and Mirjana."

"What?" said Ivo.

"Really?" asked Amir.

"Yes. They are my close friends ever since grade school and they have told me everything about the visions."

Tony's eye widened till they nearly fell out. A flash of chills hit him and his heart began to race. This was it. This was the answer to his prayers.

CHAPTER 9

THE FINAL PROPHECY

Thursday, 7:00pm

"Did you just say: *your friends since grade school?*" repeated the professor in astonishment.

"Yes. I grew up in Medjugorje. When my Mama die, Papa move us here."

Holy Christ! Thought Tony. *She is the real deal.* Suddenly, his whole world brightened. She just might be a dream come true. He needed to keep her talking.

"Wow!" said Tony. "This could add a totally new angle to my movie!"

"Slow down," said the Serb, "This is complete nonsense. Pure fiction." But his incredulity was not shared by any of the others.

"Marija, tell us more!" said Ivo, pulling up a chair next to her.

"The secrets, Marija! Tell us about the secrets," said the professor, impatiently. Tony looked at him and saw that his eyes were nearly popping out of his head. His face was almost maniacal.

"Well, the ten secrets given to the children are far beyond our human understanding," said Marija.

"Can you give us an example?" said Tony.

She paused for a moment and closed her eyes in deep thought.

"Well...the first secret says the reason God is taking so much time for the messages to appear is so that all mankind may come to conversion."

The men just listened. "And...another says that one secret will be a great sign on the hill that will be indestructible and beautiful. The sign will appear in such a way that unbelievers won't have words to describe it. It will be something that has never been seen on earth before. So of course, at this moment, it is not something that we can understand."

"I'm confused," said Tony.

"My English is not good?"

"No, no, no, you're doing wonderfully!" said the professor. "But Marija, why would Our Lady offer us this great gift, these messages, and then not tell us how to understand them? To use them?"

Marija smiled a broad and knowing smile. "Mirjana asked the Lady just such a question! And the Lady tell her to choose a priest to help reveal the secrets to the world."

"And did she?" asked Ivo.

"Yes, years ago, Mirjana chose Father Petar Ljubicic to help reveal the secrets to the world."

"And has he?"

"No."

"Why not?" asked Tony.

"Because it is not time yet. Father Petar will only read each secret ten days before it is to occur. During that time, he must fast for the first seven days. And then, three days before the secret happens, he will announce it to the world."

Tony remembered reading something about this in one of his books. He didn't quite understand it then and he didn't understand it now.

"Marija, seven days, ten days, three days, this is all very confusing. Do you think you could get me an interview with this priest? Perhaps he can explain it," asked Tony.

"I don't think so. I don't think he…"

"What about the kids?" interrupted Tony. "Is there a way to reach them?"

"Will you please shut up for one minute and let her go on!" growled the professor.

"No, no, that is all right. I need to get back to work now," said Marija.

"No! No! Please, no!" they all implored.

"But my father will get angry with me."

"We will explain it to him!" said Amir.

"And leave a big tip!" added Tony.

"Marija, let me ask you one more question. Did the lady tell your friends anything else that none of you have ever told the reporters or anyone?" asked the professor. "Are there any references, any mentions of the miracles?"

She bit her lip and thought for a minute, "I think no… not really."

The Serb laughed at them. "Are you all done? This is a waste of time."

"Hey it doesn't cost you anything to listen!" said Ivo. "Show some respect."

But it seemed that Marija had said pretty much all she had to say. As soon as it was clear that in terms of big revelations, this was approaching a dead end, they started to heave heavy sighs of disappointment. They were all still captivated by the girl and her story, but it appeared that she had little really new information to shed light on.

Tony still wanted to pick her brain, because he was sure she knew intimate little details that none of the books on Medjugorje contained and that information alone might be worth something. He was reaching for a business card to give her when suddenly, inexplicably, she lit up like a beacon. Her eyes were full and bright and she looked breathless. She stood up.

"Wait!" she said, "There is something."

"Yes?" said Tony.

"Something we talk about, not exactly in the messages, but about the…um…the nature of the messages?"

"What do you mean?" asked Tony.

"No, no! That's good! That's very good!" said the professor. "What was it?"

"Well," she paused as if to gather her thoughts and decide how to put it. "You see, after a while, we began to notice that people stop calling the messages: visions… and they start to call them 'miracles.' You see?"

"Ah! Interesting! Yes?"

"But, of course, we never thought of them as miracles! They were very natural things to us. But, once the word 'miracle' began to be used in the newspaper, the children began to get letters from all around the world; from sick people asking for the children to pray for them. Asking to mention them to the Lady. It was crazy. It was all too much. Because, it was not our place, you see. Her messages were, had, um, *bigger* importance?"

"Ah! So the idea of addressing temporal things seemed inconsequential?" asked the professor.

Marija just stared at him. "Please?"

Amir jumped into action and spoke in Bosnian to her suggesting, "The lady's messages were for all mankind and not individual men?"

"Yes! Exactly!" she said.

"Marija, have you ever been interviewed by anyone about this?" asked Tony.

"Oh yes, years ago, but after a while, no one really cares anymore."

"Holy 'exclusive,' Batman!" said Tony.

"What else was there, Marija? What were you about to say? Is there anything else, any other secrets that the world doesn't know about?"

She looked around and fidgeted, appearing afraid to be breaking some kind of confidence.

"There are many," she said.

"What do you mean?" said Amir.

"The Ten Great Secrets which the Lady told the children were meant for all mankind, but not every secret was meant for the whole world."

"What does that mean?" asked Tony.

"What I mean is, some of the secrets were very personal, for the children themselves and no one else."

"Really? This is extraordinary!" said the professor. "I never read about any of this!"

Tension was beginning to show on Marija's face and perspiration appeared on her brow. Tony worried that she was about to cut them off. He decided to roll the dice and go for the throat.

"Marija, the secrets. Do you know these secrets? Did they share them with you?" he asked.

Marija appeared to be hyperventilating and suddenly bolted back behind the counter. Her eyes had the fear of God in them.

"I have said too much! I have to get back to work now," she said.

"Wait, Marija!" said Ivo.

"There is something, isn't there?" said the professor.

"Come on Marija! You can't leave us hanging like this!" said Tony.

"No. Father will be angry! Business is bad and I am not supposed to talk to the customers too much."

"Marija, your father won't be angry. We'll make sure of it!" said the professor.

"Absolutely! I promise you!" said Tony, realizing that the decision was cutting her up inside. It had to be big.

She looked in the kitchen. "Where is my father?"

"He's upstairs."

She took a deep cleansing breath. "OK, but as soon as you hear him start to come, tell me! He would beat me if he knew I was talking about this to strangers." They sat in solemn silence as she walked around the counter and sat among them. Never did any sage possess more attentive and acutely focused disciples.

She let out another deep cleansing breath, a breath that seemed to carry the weight of the world within it.

"Well, as you have guessed. There is... something else."

"I knew it!" said the professor.

"What? What is it?" asked Ivo.

"It is just that," she bit her lip and wrung her hands nervously, "...the secrets that the lady tells to the children, they are meant only for the children. They are private."

"But they told them to you," said the professor.

"Yes, but they tell me in confidence. I feel guilty already for talking about it. And my father will kill me if he knows this is what we are speaking about."

She looked like she would cry and Tony started to panic. If she shut down now he might never get her talking like this again. He decided to roll the dice again and lay it on heavy.

"Marija, listen," he said solemnly, "I realize this is hard for you and you feel that in some way you are betraying your friends confidence, but I assure you, it is never a sin to spread the word of God."

"I am going to be sick," said the Serb.

"Marija," Tony continued. "If you know something important, something that may benefit the whole world, you have an obligation, a sacred duty to share it."

"Stop it!" yelled the Serb. "Leave the damn girl alone!"

"Stay out of this!" said Ivo.

"No! I will not. Have your moronic little fantasy, but stop beating up the child!"

"This is no concern of yours," said Amir.

"And what concern is it of yours? You're Muslim. What do you care about Christian mythology?"

"None of your Goddamn business, Chetnik!" said Amir.

"Stop! Please! Stop!" cried Marija. "This is exactly the trouble since the day the visions started! They were meant only for good, but whenever they are discussed, nothing good ever happens. This is why I believe we are not ready for these messages yet. I speak no more until I have your promise, no more fighting!"

They settled down, looked at one another and nodded in agreement.

"We promise."

Marija again looked as if she was carrying the weight of the entire world on her shoulders. Just discussing the visions was physically exhausting to her.

"Would you like some water?" offered Tony.

"No. I am fine. But thank you. You are very kind." She closed her eyes and folded her hands in front of her then spoke very deliberately. "Very well. I will tell you something that I have told no one else in my life. It was shared with me just after Our Lady gave Mirjana the tenth and final secret."

Upstairs the floorboards creaked and she looked startled. She put a finger to her lip and rushed to the bottom of the stairs. When she was convinced her father was not coming she went behind the counter and shut the kitchen door. Then she walked over and sat between the two tables the men were assembled at. She bid them all to come closer.

"It is well known that the only physical proof of the visions is the parchment left by our Lady containing the ten secrets."

"Wait a minute. You mean to say, the Virgin Mary actually gave the children a parchment? A real, physical, tangible parchment?" said the professor.

"Yes," said Marija.

Tony felt the hairs on his neck standing on edge. Electricity fired through his veins.

"And, who has that parchment today?" asked Tony.

"Mirjana gave it to Father Petar."

"Does he still have it? Has he shown it to anyone?" asked Tony.

"I believe he still has it. Its contents are well known." Marija leaned forward and with a sly smile continued. "But...the message that accompanied the parchment, the final prophecy, has never ever been disclosed."

They looked at her in astonishment.

"A spoken message?" asked the professor.

"Yes. On the day the Lady gave the children the tenth and final secret, and left behind the only physical... um ...*evidence*? The proof that she was real and not imagined or just a dream. On that day, the Lady spoke for the first and only time about mankind's need for peace. She spoke of the many kinds of peace that exist in the kingdom of heaven. Physical peace, peace of mind, peace of spirit. And she said that to find peace, man first needed to heal himself."

"Heal himself? Of what? Of mental anguish? Of temptation? Of what?" asked the professor.

"Mirjana would never ever try to explain the meaning of any of the messages. She believed it was not our place to do so. She thought she was only to repeat them. But one evening, while we were going for a walk, Ivanka spoke to me of what she believed was the meaning of the messages. She said she thought they were dangerous. I asked her *what did she mean*? Dangerous? And that is when she told me of the final message, the one that accompanied the 10th secret, which was till then unknown."

"But you just said..." said Amir.

"Ssssh! Don't interrupt her! Go on!" said Ivo.

"She said that she believed that this last message was meant to be taken on many levels, in both spiritual and physical. Well, this did not sound like the Ivanka I knew at all! She was always a very simple girl. Where could these deep thoughts be coming from? Her words confused me, so I went home that night and prayed for her. The next day we met again and I asked her about the message, but she told me she had no idea what I was talking about. I told her she was being mean to me and to stop joking. But it was as if the entire conversation had never happened."

"But the message?" implored the professor. "What about the message?"

"I couldn't stop thinking about what she said and I was very worried about her. So, I went to church to pray and lit a candle for her."

She paused and opened her eyes wide, looking positively rapturous. A cavernous hush came over the room and a beatific light came into her face and her eyes began to tear up.

"And that was when it happened!" she said.

"What? What happened?" begged Tony.

"As I struck the match to light the candle, foolishly I let the match burn all the way down. It burned my fingers and I cried out. The pain was terrible, so I ran to the stream behind the church to cool my fingers in the water. The cold water quickly eased my pain, but when I took my hand out, soon the pain returned. So, I put my hand back into the stream and I thought, if only I could keep my hand in the stream until it was healed. And then I remembered the message..."

She slowly got to her feet and looked as if she was reading off some great invisible sign in the distance. She reached out her hand as if to touch it.

"The message that came with the tenth secret...about man's need for healing. It suddenly seemed so clear to me...what if, what if the message was not a mystery at all? What if healing simply meant... *healing*? Simple physical healing? Because, remember, many, many people were being healed from all kinds of sickness and disease just by visiting the shrine. Maybe the message contained the... instruction? The way...something that would cure people of illness! Because that would be the most sure way to make them believe and trust and love God."

She was glowing radiantly as she spoke. She turned and looked at their spellbound faces.

"Do you understand?"

"Yes, yes, go on! Please!" cried the professor.

Tony noticed that the old professor was sweating profusely. His face was bright red.

"I went home and I think about the message all that night... when suddenly...I saw it!"

Suddenly, she seemed to go into a trance. Once again she appeared to be looking into the distance and reached out to touch something. Tears began to form at the corners of her eyes. They were the tears of ecstasy.

"The Lady's words. The final message: 'And through these words, all things will be made well!'" She paused and a great beaming smile came to her face. It was almost as if she was aglow.

Tony felt his heart stir like it had never done before. This girl. She was shattering his belief system, setting something in motion deep within him. He felt that his place in the order of the universe was about to change and his reason for living was being redefined.

"It was so obvious that no one could see it. I was positive I was right, and I ran and told Mirjana and Ivanka!" Suddenly the smile disappeared. "But they scolded me so viciously they made me cry. I was so upset I didn't speak to them for days. They really hurt my feelings. But soon, Mirjana came to see me and she apologized. She…she gave me this cross!" She pulled out a small gold cross from under her blouse.

"It's beautiful," said Ivo.

"But she told me again, it was not for us to try to explain the Lady's messages, for if we were wrong…we would be spreading lies in the Lady's name. And we would suffer eternal damnation. She make me promise never to speak about it again."

"And did you?" asked Tony.

"Not until now."

"And the children?"

"I have not spoken to Mirjana or Ivanka since."

"Then the meaning of the message remains a mystery?" asked the professor sadly, almost afraid of the answer.

A tiny hint of a smile appeared on her face.

"Not exactly."

Tony felt the hairs on the back of his neck stand.

"What do you mean?" said Tony.

"I told you," she said, her smile growing. "It was so simple that a child could figure it out."

The professor leaned very close to her, his eyes growing wider.

"And you did figure it out, didn't you?"

"I knew it!" cried Ivo.

Marija stood up and stepped back from them.

"The date of the tenth secret is known only to Mirjana and Father Petar," she said. "When he announces it to the world, only then will I reveal the meaning of the hidden message. And only on that day, all of those pure of heart will be healed."

Tony's heart nearly stopped.

"Wait a minute," he said. "You mean to say, the Lady's message actually did contain a way to cure illness?"

Marija closed her eyes and solemnly nodded her head.

"Holy shit!" Tony muttered under his breath.

"Wait. Have you tried it? Does it work?" asked the professor.

"Can we see it? This message." said Amir.

"Did Mirjana and Ivanka ever figure it out?" asked Tony.

Marija shook her head. "No. They were too busy meeting with priests and politicians. No. I alone know the secret of the Gospa. The Final Prophecy."

From the bar, the Serb finally spoke up. "And why, pray tell, have you kept this marvelous story to yourself for so long?" he asked.

"Why?" she cried, her eyes full of tears and fury. She walked over to the Serb and got right in his face. "Because, one morning, out of blue, police show up at Mirjana's house and drag her away in handcuffs! They interrogate her for months. They force her to quit school. They say they will put her in mental institution unless she admits she is lying. She said: 'to know Heaven but to live on Earth is pain that no one else can imagine.'"

"Did she give in eventually?" asked Tony.

"Never. They promised Mirjana that she could go to best school, have great job, her family could have any house they want, if only she would say it is all a big lie— but she would not. I think the Lady chose her because she was so strong. I was not as strong as her and I didn't want to go through that, so I keep silent!"

She walked back to her chair and sat back down.

"Besides, I cannot do anything with the secret until Father Petar makes his announcement. That is the way it must be. That is what the Lady wanted. But, on that day...on *that day*, I will show the children and everyone else that I was right and they were wrong!"

"Marija, please show us!" said Ivo.

"Yes, please! It would mean so much!" said the professor.

Only Tony could see she was hesitant to say anymore, something was bothering her. But this was not the time for silence, she was on a roll and Tony knew this opportunity might not happen twice. He needed a little bit of good luck for once. He was really pushing it, but he played the emotional card one more time.

"Marija," he said tenderly. "I know you feel the secret is sacred and in a way magical. But, telling us how it works won't make it any less sacred or magical. It will still be…a miracle. Is there some reason you don't want to show us?"

"I told you, there is nothing to show," she said. "It is not written anywhere."

"What?" asked Tony.

"I told you before. Once I hear these messages, I never forget them. So I never write them down."

"What!" exclaimed the professor, in a half-crazed rage. "But what if you should forget or have an injury or God-forbid something worse! The world needs to know! It's, it's irresponsible not to write it down! You must!"

She calmly folded her arms.

"I prefer not to."

The professor stood up in a rage and grabbed her by the shoulders.

"You prefer not to?! You prefer not to?!" he said shaking her violently. "Who are you, Bartleby the fucking Scrivener? Who do you think you are?"

It took a moment but the others managed to pull him off of her. Ivo threw him back into his chair which fell over backwards. No one bothered to assist him as he slowly crawled back to his seat. Marija was visibly shaken.

"Are you crazy?" Ivo screamed at the professor.

Tony embraced Marija protectively.

"But you don't understand!" said the professor.

"Shut up or I'll kick your teeth out! Just sit there!" cried Ivo.

"Are you okay, sweetie?" asked Tony.

"I'm fine. But you see? Once again, where ever the secrets go, violence follows. We are not ready for them. Our Lady said, 'Only the pure of heart could see her and hear her.'"

"But the lady must have meant for you to share it!" said the professor, "Why else would she possibly have told you? Don't you see, my dear, you may be holding the key to eternity in your hand!"

"Sir, I believe the Lord Jesus and the Lady have brought you all here for a reason. But you must search your heart to find that reason, remember the Lady's words: Only the pure of heart will..."

"Yes, yes, the pure of heart, that's fine!" said Tony. "But all that matters is that you're alright."

His words had a soothing effect and she began to settle down.

"I am fine," she said. "Thank you."

Amir stood up and paced around the perimeter of the room with his hands on his head in shock.

Just then, Tony unleashed a masterstroke. He looked deeply into her eyes.

"Marija, you know, that's a pretty awesome responsibility to carry on your little shoulders," he said. "So, I just want you to know, that if you ever feel the burden is too great, we're here for you. If you want to discuss it, fine. If not, well, that's OK, too." As he said this, he tucked her hair behind her ears and caressed her cheek reassuringly.

"Thank you," she said.

"Tony."

"Thank you, Tony. You have kind eyes."

"*Molim, draga, molim,*" he said.

She hugged him. He held her in his arms in a deep embrace. He could feel her heart racing like a humming bird against his chest. His instinctive conviction was that she was the real deal. His own heart was filled with compassion, but also with a nagging sense of impatience right along side it. Over her shoulder, he winked at the other guys.

Just then, the old man strolled down the steps waving a deck of cards. When he saw Tony with his arms around his daughter he went berserk. He rushed behind the counter, reached beneath it and pulled out a shotgun. He pointed it at Tony and started screaming in Bosnian.

When the rest of the pilgrims saw the shotgun chaos ensued. As the professor pleaded with the old man, like a cat, Ivo lunged at him and grabbed the barrel of the gun. They struggled but Ivo easily overpowered the old man—but not before he got off a shot which blew a hole in the plaster ceiling. Finally, once they wrestled the gun away from him things settled down.

Amir and the professor tried to calm down the irate old man but had little success. He screamed at his daughter.

"Marija! Go!" he said and she ran through the door behind the counter to the kitchen, but she paused momentarily and smiled at Tony. It did not go unnoticed.

"You! I swear to God! You touch my daughter again, I kill you!"

As they again calmed the old man down, Tony was staring at the hole in the ceiling.

"Holy shit. That guy is fucking crazy!" he said.

"Okay, okay. It's all right! Relax!" yelled Ivo, as he led the old man away behind the counter. The old man shook loose of Ivo's grip and he went after his daughter, watching Tony over his shoulder all the way.

Stunned silence filled the room. They began to sit at a table to decompress from the violence and take in everything they'd just learned. The professor stood and leaned against the bar. Amir paced about nervously. Only the Serb seemed completely unperturbed by the events. He lit another cigarette and took a long drag. If anything, he looked amused by the situation.

"This changes matters somewhat, doesn't it?" he said with a laugh.

CHAPTER 10

THE ENIGMA

Thursday, 7:30pm

"It's a miracle!" cried Ivo.

"This girl has absolutely no idea what she's sitting on here!" said Tony. "This could be the message the whole world's been waiting for!"

"It's a miracle!" repeated Ivo.

"It was already delivered and no one even noticed it!" said Tony.

"It's a miracle," said Ivo again, like a mantra.

"Think of the historical implications," said Amir

"And it's all ours!" said Tony.

'Think of the odds!" said Amir.

"The what?" said Tony.

"Don't you see? The ethnic composition. All of our faiths are represented here, none can claim the discovery for themselves."

"The ethnic composition?" said a bewildered Tony.

"So? What about it?" asked the Serb.

"So," said Amir, "I believe that this could not be an accident."

"Holy Shit. It's like God himself wanted us all to be here at this exact time in this exact place. It was predestined," said Ivo.

"Ooof! That just gave me goose bumps! But I wouldn't worry boys, if we're right, there'll be plenty to go around!" said Tony.

"Plenty of what?" asked Ivo.

"And you called me retarded? Money, you idiot! This could mean a fortune. A fortune! Two simple words: miracle cure!"

"Money?" said Ivo. "Don't you understand what we talking about? What we are dealing with?"

Tony looked at Ivo like he had three heads, but this was not the time to get all high and mighty.

"Wait! Slow down a minute," said Amir pacing rapidly back and forth. "Let's not get ahead of ourselves." He glanced over at the professor who was staring silently into space and walked over to him. "I can't believe *you're* being so quiet. I thought you'd be bursting!"

"Yeah, not acting like some kind of nut," said Ivo.

The professor heaved a great sigh and stood up. He rubbed his hands on his pants, then he rubbed his eyes. He looked at them all as if he was looking right through them. His entire manner had changed.

"You all thrill with the excitement of the situation, as is rightly so, and are breathless with anticipation of triumph and the riches it promises," he said. "My opinion...as a historian, I am astounded." Then he looked directly at the Serb. "As a former Rabbi..." He paused to let the words sink in. "I am skeptical." He walked to the back of the room toward the bathroom where he stopped. "But as a man dying of cancer... I am hopeful."

CHAPTER 11

THE PLAN

Thursday, 8:00pm

After a moment of stunned silence, Tony cleared his throat loudly and looked around at the mass of uncomfortable faces.

"Well, I guess that explains that," he said matter-of-factly. "Okay, let's give the guy a little slack. He's clearly got a lot on his mind."

He stood up and walked over to the bar and leaned against it. He knew that this was a critical time. He needed to take a bit more control over the situation, but he needed to do it gently. He walked over between the tables and began to lobby his constituents.

"Okay, now that we know what's been bothering him, we can understand his behavior a little bit better. So, let's all make an effort to give him a wide berth and not argue with him. He's got troubles enough."

They all nodded in agreement and Tony grabbed the moment.

"But, not to sound completely cold and callous, we need to remain focused. And frankly, all that matters right now is the girl. And how we get her to tell us what she knows."

"I'm not sure it is right that we learn it at all," said Amir firmly.

"And why the hell not?" said Tony, a bit more harshly than he'd wanted to.

"If we believe that Marija is correct, and that the message is what she says it is... and that the Lady is in fact the Blessed Virgin, should we not honor her wish and wait for the appointed date?"

The Serb stood up and walked over to Amir.

"To quote our Jewish friend," said the Serb. "I believe I speak for everyone here when I say: *fuck no*! We should make every effort to learn the secret. Then, we can decide what to do with it." He laughed. "Besides, it's probably bullshit anyway."

"I totally disagree," said Tony. "I think she's the real deal. Did you get a look at her? It was like she was channeling another world. And she knows all kinds of things and details that they don't even mention in any of the books! No, I believe her."

"Me too!" said Ivo. "I get a very good feeling from her!"

"And to answer your question," said Tony, "of course we're gonna share it. We have to! The whole world will benefit. Think of it!"

"Of course you say that!" said Amir. "You've suddenly got a gold mine of a movie script laid at your feet! A miraculous story!"

"Movie script?" said Tony incredulously. "You gotta be kidding me! Don't you get it? If even one single person is cured by Marija's discovery, we're rich beyond our wildest dreams! All of us!"

"How?" said the Croat.

"Do I have to paint a sign? Once word gets out, and you know it will, we'll be overwhelmed with offers! The drug companies alone will pay millions just to keep it off the market!"

"Why would anyone want to keep a miracle cure *off* the market?" asked the Croat.

"Because, soon we'll be eating their lunch, that's why! It happens every day."

"Fuck that shit!" said Ivo. "If we can help people with cancer, we have to. We *have* to!"

Ivo was starting to get under Tony's skin. Who would have guessed that the kid had so many scruples?

"And what if Marija should say that she will tell us the secret only on the condition that we not reveal it to anyone? What then?" asked Amir.

Before anyone could answer, the professor suddenly reappeared, looking weary and a bit contrite.

"I want to apologize for my behavior…"

"Don't worry. Say no more. It's okay." They reassured him.

"In that case," he said, heaving a great sigh, "I suppose we need to have a serious talk. Let's proceed."

He came around and sat at a table with Ivo and Amir.

"First of all, I overheard much of what you were saying while I was in the men's room and I must say this: in my opinion, these children, the visionaries, their behavior, they do not strike me as zealots, or as activists. They are not beating anyone over the head and demanding that they are telling the truth. They aren't going around trying to convert people. They simply deliver their messages and get on with their lives. To me, that makes them very believable. And if we believe what we've just heard from Marija, then we have to ask ourselves, and let us all respond with a show of hands—who believes that she is telling the truth?"

Tony was astonished to see that every hand was raised, even that of the Serb.

"But, let me clarify if I may," said the Serb.

"For Christ's sake!" said Ivo. "It's a simple yes or no answer!"

"No, it is not!" insisted the Serb. "I do not believe that Mary, the mother of God, has conversations with ignorant country girls about the end of the world or miracle cures for disease. I wouldn't believe it if the child developed stigmata! What I do believe…is that *she believes* she is telling the truth, but not necessarily that she is correct."

"The Qur'an tells us it is the message and not the messenger that matters. You're *afraid* it's true!" said Amir. "You're afraid because if it is true, then you and your people will have a lot of reckoning to do!"

Tony decided it was time to take hold of the situation and lead. He clapped his hands loudly to draw their attention.

"Okay, focus guys!" he said. "Now listen, if we can get her to talk tonight, we can still make it to Medjugorje by tomorrow. And if so, maybe we could ask the Lady herself to explain the mystery to the children!"

"But hasn't she already explained it?" said Amir. "In the way she wanted it to be known. Can we really be so presumptuous as to ask the Mother of God to explain herself to the likes of us?" They sat in silence and pondered. "And you still haven't answered my question. What if Marija will only tell us the secret on the condition that we not reveal it to anyone? What then?" asked Amir. "We certainly cannot compel her to tell us—the very stones would cry out against it!"

They were stuck again. Tony could see that the Bosnian kid was gripped with doubt, and that this doubt, while genuine, seemed grossly disproportionate to the situation. This was not good news.

He needed to get in line and quick. Tony could deal with Ivo, but if both he and Amir started in with the guilt that would be real trouble. The stones might cry out against it, but even stones get worn down over time by the flow of water. Tony had to be firm, but patient.

"I don't believe that every puzzle is meant to be solved; some are intended to remain a mystery," said Amir.

"That's just nonsense!" said Tony.

"No it is not! It says in the Qur'an: 'To Allah belongeth the mysteries of the heavens and the earth; for Allah hath power over all things.'"

"He's right, you know," said Ivo. "He's completely right. Besides, I wasn't going to Medjugorje to cure anything. I was just going to offer my confession."

"I'm not Catholic, but can't you just do that in any church?" asked Tony.

"Perhaps our Croatian friend has great sins to atone for?" said the Serb.

Ivo looked at the Serb and appeared ready to punch his lights out again. But instead, he took out his cigarettes and lit one.

"My sins are my business as are my reasons to visit Medjugorje. I am content to wait."

The professor stood and scratched his chin.

"With all due respect, I am afraid I do not agree with my Muslim friend in this matter. I do not believe, nor do I accept that the same God who has endowed us with sense, reason, and intellect intends for us to completely forgo their use."

Thank God! Finally, somebody was making sense, thought Tony. The professor, who had been a constant thorn in his side so far, might actually become an ally after all.

"I completely agree," said Tony. "And frankly, I think it's an insult to God not to use all our gifts to their greatest capacity! Right?"

The Serb chuckled softly to himself, "Yes, I completely agree. Although, it does sound a little bit funny coming out of your mouth."

"Okay, as time is short for us, let's continue, please," said the professor.

"Wait, why exactly is time so short for us anyway?" asked Ivo.

"Haven't I explained that already?" said Tony.

"No. Time is short for *you*! Not for us. *We* have plenty of time."

Tony narrowed his eyes and bit his lip.

"Let's stay focused please," said the professor. "Now, this is important, Marija said, the Lady could only be seen and heard by the pure of heart. Well, that pretty much counts all of us out. So, I propose that we..."

"Hey! Wait! That's not fair!" they protested.

"Do we really believe we are so spotless as to stand before the Mother of God?" said the professor. "I believe if we really wish to understand the message, we must at the very least begin by being completely honest with ourselves. Marija could not have been more clear about this. We should begin by explaining our intentions in going to Medjugorje, then we can decide whether or not..."

But before he could finish his sentence, the door flew open and the driver's assistant came in from the rain. He was full of energy. The driver, who had been sitting in the corner, blissfully unconcerned with all the drama going on around him, took his headphones off to hear the news.

"Good news! The road's clear. We can get going."

"Okay, everybody," said the driver, "five minutes and we go!"

A pang of terror filled Tony and a thousand thoughts filled his head in an instant. He couldn't possibly leave now. But he was due to fly in two days. But this was a possible life-changer; he had to see it through. He looked around at his colleagues and saw similar concerns in their eyes.

The driver stood up and put on his coat, and then he left with his assistant. The men panicked.

"Crap! Now what do we do?" said Tony.

"Well, we could stay the night, they do have rooms," said the professor.

"But the Virgin is coming tomorrow!" said Ivo.

"She's there every month, same time, same hill," said the Serb.

"Yes, but Mirjana isn't! And neither am I," said Tony.

"It's funny how life sometimes gives us exactly what we have been asking for just when we need it the least," said the Serb, with a loud cackle of laughter.

"Where do you get your sick philosophy? Did you read it in a fortune cookie?" asked Tony. The Serb was beyond getting on his nerves.

"Hey!" called out Amir, getting their attention. "Okay, quickly now, what are our options?"

"It's quite simple," said the professor. "We could go and hope to see the Virgin appear tomorrow or we can stay and try to convince Marija that our motives are pure and to share her secret with us."

"We could split up. Half go and half stay here?" said Ivo.

"No, no, no, no," said the Serb. "We all stick together. I mean no disrespect but...I don't trust a single one of you."

"Can't we do both? Can't we get a car tomorrow to take us?" said Tony.

"A car? This isn't New York. You can't just call a taxi," said the professor.

"Look, there's no time, we have to decide now." said Amir.

"Well, we could wait here and come back next month to see the Virgin. I wouldn't mind seeing Marija again; she's cute," said Ivo.

"Sure, I'll just hop another plane from LA!" said Tony. "Look, let's be practical for a second—most of the visions seem to me to be just new age nonsense, but tomorrow, Mirjana's going to be there, for the first time in years! If ever there was a time to be in Medjugorje...I'm afraid it's tomorrow."

"If only we knew for sure that Marija will tell us," said Ivo.

Tony's head was throbbing. He wanted to stay, but he wasn't sure he'd crack Marija anytime soon. On the other hand, Mirjana was a sure bet to be there; it was in all the papers. Then again, even if he did get Marija to tell him the secret, there was no way to be sure it really worked! What if she was wrong!

"I bet she's already tried it!" he said with a burst of energy. "That's the only explanation! She was way too confident! She must know already that it works!"

"She never exactly told us what *it* is," pointed out Amir.

"She never had the chance! Martin Scorsese here wouldn't shut the fuck up for two seconds to let her speak!" said the Serb.

"Hey!"

"So busy trying to calculate ways to best exploit her!"

"Whoa!" said Tony. "That is so not fair! If you think I'm somehow soiling everything, let me just say that up to this moment, I'm the only one here who's been completely fucking honest! Okay? And why the fuck should I answer to you? I don't know you. You haven't told us one goddamn thing about yourself. You could be a fucking child-molesting war criminal for all we know!"

The Serb let out a huge yawn, "Not that any of this matters. I've seen many of these country girls before, all silly religious zealots. It could take days for her to debate and decide and we still don't know she'll decide in our favor. I say…"

Suddenly, Marija appeared on the stairs.

"Tony?" she said.

He stood up and ran to her. "Marija! Are you okay? What is it?"

She took a deep breath and spoke. "I have decided," she said. "I am going to tell you. I will write it down. For you."

The men were literally jumping for joy and they didn't bother trying to conceal it. Tony hugged her.

"But…I have to tell you," she cautioned them, "I have not thought about it for a very long time, so it will take a while to write it down. I don't want to make any mistakes."

"That's okay! That's okay!" he said. "Take your time!" He motioned to the rest of them. "And if you need anything from us we'll be down here waiting."

"Marija?" asked the Serb in a saccharin sweet voice. "Do you really believe all this?"

The question infuriated Ivo, who looked like he might kill the Serb. Marija just looked confused.

"I'm sorry. I don't understand. Do I believe what?"

"All of this, the visions, the Virgins, the messages?"

Her face, which never looked more childlike, suddenly began to change. She slowly looked upward and solemn tears began to form at the corners of her eyes.

"Sir, when I was very young in Catholic School, they taught us to believe in miracles. As I have grown older, I hear there are no more miracles, some say there really never were any. But the day the Gospa gave Mirjana the tenth and final secret, I was there at Crnica. I know you think I am a simple and stupid country girl, but I saw with my own eyes the clouds part and the full moon pour its light on the children. It was beautiful more than I can describe. And what I saw with my eyes, and what I heard with my ears, and what I felt in my heart; it was not of this world."

They all fell silent.

"I should go," said Marija.

Tony gently took her hand and through tear-filled eyes and choking on his words he said, "God bless you, Marija."

She squeezed his hands. "Thank you, Tony." She turned and started to leave, but stopped.

"What is it? What's the matter?" he asked. Suddenly she spun around and threw her arms around him and kissed him. He was completely shocked. It took a minute but he managed to gently pull her off.

"Hey! Hey! Wait! Stop! You father! Your father!"

"Don't worry about him!" she said.

"Marija! Please! There's time for all this later." She nodded and stepped back. "Now we have work to do." He winked at her. She smiled and quickly departed up the stairs, skipping away like a girl in love.

Tony let out a sign of relief; one big land mine avoided, at least for the time being. He faced the rest of the pilgrims.

"Well gentlemen, I'd say our chances just got a heck of a lot better!" he said.

"What's your wife going to say?" said Ivo, disapprovingly.

"Oh stop it, Ivo. Just taking one for the team. You all should be thanking me!"

"I think it must be his *kind eyes,*" said the professor.

The bus driver poked his head in from the rain. "Okay, everybody going to Medjugorje. Bus is leaving now!" He departed and the sound of the bus' ignition roared in the parking lot.

"It's now or never," said Amir.

A moment of tense silence filled the room again. They all looked with searching eyes around at one another.

"Well, they say, when Caesar crossed the Rubicon, he burned the bridges behind him. I believe we must do the same," said the professor.

Tony nodded in agreement and bellied up to the bar.

"Okay, listen up," said Tony, "if we stay, we gotta agree, we work together. No bullshit, no funny stuff! Got it? We don't have to be friends and we don't even have to like each other, but for the next twenty-four hours we're a team. Agreed?"

"Shall we have a show of hands?" said the professor. "All in favor of staying?"

For the second time that evening, every hand went up. And outside, the bus horn beeped and the engine could be heard pulling out of the parking lot onto the road to Medjugorje.

"No turning back now!" said Tony gravely.

"Must everything be a movie to you?" said the professor.

Tony smiled and winked at him.

"Whenever possible," he said with a laugh. "Aaaaaand scene!"

"Jesus, help us," said the Serb. "Where's the old man? I'm starving. Surely he must have something not in cellophane for dinner!"

CHAPTER 12

A LITTLE TOUCH OF TONY IN THE NIGHT

Friday, 2:15am

Tony tossed and turned in the lumpy bed but could find no rest. When he couldn't sleep, his mind raced in hundreds of seemingly disconnected directions, from one topic to another and back again.

Both his primary and secondary plans for the trip were in shambles. Tuzla had been a disaster and researching an indie film, hoping that the hot topic of Bosnia might get him some notice and possibly a distribution deal was now a distant memory. This girl was troubling him to his soul. He realized that he was capable of some really rotten things, and she reminded him of that—*thanks!* This country was a complex combination of contradictions to him. It was the most singularly beautiful place he'd ever seen and yet some of the worst atrocities in human history happened here, right under the noses of the western world. He really didn't want to think about that stuff anymore, he'd seen and heard enough in just a week to last him a lifetime. And the faces of the children he'd met in Tuzla would stay with him for a lifetime as well. Unfortunately, so would the faces of the politicians and administrators who had dashed his dreams with their greed and treachery.

The children of Medjugorje were Marija's childhood friends. Imagine the irony. The fact that the very rest area which they'd stopped in was her home; it was all too much to believe. He was never very lucky, at least up till this point in his life; in fact, he often thought of himself as the least lucky person on earth. He struggled constantly to scrape out a living while friends of his—far less talented friends—far less intelligent friends—were making fortunes turning out complete and utter shit. It made him crazy. But that would all change now, and Marija held the key. Her childhood friends had shared an intimate secret with her and she was going to give it to him. The secret of the Gospa.

Tony retained no friends from childhood himself, but he imagined that if he had, that they'd be the kind that would share even the most intimate secrets; secrets that could rock and change the fate of the world.

His only regret was that Claire wasn't here to share it. This was also his first trip without her doing the planning and packing for him and in that respect, it was a sobering lesson in his own inadequacy. He thought of her constantly; from the airport, to the flight—his only ever trans-Atlantic flight on his own; to the visit to the home in Tuzla. It was her idea to visit in the first place, but it became his passion and soon after, it became his ruin. He obsessed on the kids. After having spent time playing with them and sharing a bond beyond description, it was extremely difficult to just return to his bourgeois nine to five existence. Working with the children gave him a sense of satisfaction, pride, and joy with which nothing he'd done in his life up to that point could compare.

One problem was that he couldn't accurately describe the experience or the feeling to his friends or family. They simply looked at him and nodded like he was crazy as he cried and went on and on with his stories. Worse yet, was the feeling that everything he did since, both personally and professionally, seemed incredibly pointless after working with the children. It enriched his life beyond words but gave him a tremendous handicap as well. He often joked that spending time working at the orphanage was the best and the worst thing he'd ever done in his life. He hoped the opportunity would arise when he could tell Amir just how much the home in Tuzla meant to him.

Secretly, he also hoped that the events of the coming morning would be something that he could tell Claire with pride and return to share with her triumphantly. He knew it sounded silly, but whenever she told him she was proud of him, it was the greatest feeling he'd ever known. He remembered how she'd told him that, until he came along, love was simply an abstract concept, meant for someone else and not her. *How could you* not *love that?*

She was his whole world and despite all, he knew he was losing her. Getting bad news back at the orphanage had thrown his whole plan, his whole life, into disarray. He probably should have done more homework before he got on that plane to come here; 20/20 hindsight, but that had always been his style, and his downfall.

"We are terribly sorry, Mr. Marshall, but I am afraid you've made a long journey for nothing." The words reverberated in his brain. The only thing that made him angrier was the hanging question they'd left him with about "giving them a reason to look the other way." He understood it only too well. This was a kleptocracy. He had been warned of it and still it caught him by surprise at the least opportune moment. The travel agent had told him to expect it, admonishing him: "In Bosnia, when the officials *stop* taking bribes, that's when you need to worry!"

Unfortunately, at this moment, he was not in financial shape to play their game. He was shattered by the news, but initially he determined not to let it derail him. Up untill recently, he knew his greatest strength was that he never gave up. But lately, he'd had so much shit in his life that he was just about ready to cash out. Until Marija.

This girl and her secret would be the ticket. It had to be.

He rolled over and looked at the old professor, who, just before turning in for the night, finally shared his name with Tony. If he was trying to keep his faith a secret, it was clear that the name Itzak was not going to be helpful. Yet Tony couldn't imagine why he'd want to keep it a secret? Nobody over here was anti-Semitic. *Were they?* In fact, it seemed to him that it was just about the only religion that wasn't hated by somebody over here. This whole place was spilling over with arcane secrets and every time you figured out one, another appeared. But he didn't have time to worry about that or argue, there were much bigger fish to fry tonight.

Itzak slept restlessly but at least he slept and Tony was jealous. He gazed at Itzak for a moment and thought, *here sleeps a man with so much learning and so little understanding.*

The ability to sleep was one of life's greatest blessings. Claire was a beautiful sleeper. Her chest rose up and fell with a gentle purr like a big sleepy cat. Sleeping next to her gave him a sense of calm and peace. Even when life was at its blackest, she was his rock. In the nearly six years since he had had a drink or done drugs, his life had achieved balance. Not a perfectly steady balance but he did own a house, have a reasonably steady income, and overall, his outlook on life was more positive than it had been in ages.

That balance came at a price, and the price was dogged, constant vigilance and an unwavering support system in the person of Claire.

The morning she left, he didn't even need to open his eyes to know she wasn't next to him. Her life force was gone from their bed. The house was total silence. He knew there was no point in searching, and he had no desire to read any note she might have left—if she even chose to leave one.

On Tony's birthday he fell off the wagon and got stinking drunk for the first time in many years. Claire didn't drink and he didn't like to drink alone so over time he had become a teetotaler. But the alcohol freed his mind and cleared his vision. He sat on the hood of his car alone, in the woods looking down at the lights of LA and wondered just how he'd mistakenly stumbled into this life. For it was clearly not *his* life. No, no, no. He was supposed to be a rich filmmaker by forty with a big house in Pacific Palisades, big enough for his entire family! He was supposed to have lots of beautiful kids smiling at him every day, whom he'd take to school and teach how to throw a curveball. His parents would live out their final days surrounded by and cared for by their loved ones, not the angry nurses at the home where both his parents had passed away. No, this life belonged to someone else, not him! And he needed to find a way out of it and back to the one that was intended for him. Somewhere along the way, he'd made a wrong turn, an error in judgment—not a deliberate or malicious one, but sometimes, he had learned, even unintentional mistakes required a lifetime of atonement.

Realizing sleep was not coming, Tony got up and walked over to the window. It was still raining outside but much lighter than before and the moon had actually snuck through the clouds in small patches.

He heard something outside, something resembling the ruffling of feathers. Then without warning, an owl screamed down from a tree just outside the window. It swooped down in a flash to grab its prey. One sharp squeal and it was over. The predator had taken his prey and flew off into the night. They did say that demons lurked in these woods.

Tony watched in amazement; it seemed so barbaric but at the same time, so natural. Animals couldn't compete with humans when it came to cruelty; we'd elevated it to an art form. *Was he behaving like that owl? Was it just the fulfilling of some natural order?* He hoped not. He really wanted to believe that his own designs were honorable, that he was not a complete opportunist, but in the end, he wanted the money more, he wanted his life back. It was all for a good cause, he told himself. He knew it and still he was slightly ashamed. If he'd been faced with this situation twenty years earlier he might have reacted differently, but this was now and this was real. If Marija's secret could benefit the entire world, he would make absolutely certain that everyone who could benefit from it would; he would see to it. But he was equally determined not to miss out on the potential fortune that he was sure was tied to it. Being a good guy and always doing the right thing hadn't done shit for him in his entire life. He was certain that money would open doors that he'd been unable to budge by himself. He couldn't wait to throw it in the faces of those miserable lawyers and administrators in Tuzla.

He looked at his watch and laughed at the mortal thoughts he'd entertained less than twenty four hours ago. It seemed like a lifetime ago. And Marija was the reason.

His head was spinning and he decided to go downstairs to the cafe and get something to drink. He put his socks on and slipped quietly out the door.

CHAPTER 13

MIDNIGHT CONFESSIONS

Friday, 2:30am

In the silence of the night, the rain on the roof and the windows was loud and soothing. The café was completely dark except for the glowing exit sign over the door and the hint of moonlight streaming in from the window and a tiny skylight over the tables.

Tony came down the stairs tiptoeing quietly. He felt his way in the darkness and went behind the counter. He found a glass and tried to fill it at the soda fountain, but it didn't work.

"Damn!" he whispered. "Is there a switch or something?" He looked around and found the beer tap but it didn't work either. "Doesn't anything work in this country?" He leaned back and touched the stove. "Ow! Mother fucker! Who left the stove on?"

"Sorry about that. I made coffee," said a voice in the blackness.

"Who's there?" asked Tony.

"Just me, Amir. You should put it under cold water, like Marija said."

"Jesus Amir! Why are you sitting in the dark?"

"I like the dark. I do my best thinking."

Tony came around and joined him at the table. Amir struck a match and lit the little candle on the table. Now that Tony could see him, he noticed that the Bosnian looked terribly troubled.

"Couldn't sleep either?" Tony asked.

"You try sleeping with Ivo; he snores like a horse."

"I do not!" said Ivo from the stairs as he descended. Like a homing beacon, he found the coffee pot in the darkness and poured himself a cup.

"You guys amaze me," said Tony. "You can drink coffee at this hour and still sleep?"

Ivo took a long sip and sat down next to Tony and Amir.

"You know what?" he said. "Please do not take this personally, but you have not stopped whining like a little girl since you got on the bus in Mostar: the bus has no air conditioning! The bus smells like smoke!"

"The passengers don't use deodorant!" added Tony. "You forgot that one."

"C'mon, guys! Quit it," said Amir.

"Caffeine is all in your head," said Ivo.

"Really? Then why does it give me heart palpitations? Caffeine's a drug, pal."

"On my planet caffeine is a vitamin," said Ivo.

The professor laughed quietly as he descended the stairs.

"Ah! The gentle aroma of coffee and cigarettes: the perfect repose!" he said.

"That's an old Croatian expression!" said Ivo.

"Excuse me?" said Amir. "No, it's an old Turkish proverb."

"Actually," said Tony. "I think it's an American movie."

They looked at him like he was insane.

"*Coffee & Cigarettes*? Jim Jarmusch movie? He's American; at least I think he's American?"

The professor joined them at the table and lit a cigarette. He blew a great plume of smoke into the air under the skylight.

"In America," he said, "you can buy great buckets of coffee in hundreds of different flavors—virtually every flavor except—coffee!"

"I like my coffee strong and black," said Ivo.

"Like your women?" said Tony. They all laughed except Amir.

"Actually, I do like my women like coffee," said Ivo, "hot and wet!"

"But why does it have to be so strong?" asked Tony.

"Old traditional Yugoslav way of making coffee," said Ivo.

"It's really Greek coffee," said the professor.

"You mean Turkish coffee!" said Amir.

"Well I think we can all agree it ain't American coffee!" said Tony.

"It's all the same shit," said Ivo, taking a long drag on his cigarette. "If he were here, the Serb would tell you it's Serbian coffee." He took another sip of coffee and let out a satisfied sign. "I think I would die without coffee and cigarettes. It's what separates us from the animals."

"What?" said Tony.

"Ever see an animal smoke?" asked Ivo.

"Not until now," said Tony. Ha! Two points for the American, he thought. "I'm actually quite proud of America's anti-smoking campaign, we're the first society in history to really take a stand and do something about it!"

"Not exactly," said *the professor*. "Nazi Germany had the world's strongest antismoking movement in the 1930s. Nazi leaders worried that tobacco might prove a hazard to the master race. It is a point of great irony, while Churchill, Stalin, and Roosevelt were chain smokers, the three great fascist leaders of Europe: Hitler, Mussolini, and Franco, were all non-smokers."

"What do you think it means?" asked Tony.

"Nothing really," said *the professor*. "Except, throughout history, conscience has kept a lot more people awake at night than either coffee or cigarettes!"

"Well put, Itzak," said Tony.

"Itzak?" said Ivo, "I thought your name was Bob?"

Itzak burst out laughing. Amir didn't laugh. He stood up and lit another cigarette. Itzak watched him and studied his expression.

"They say that if the simple things in life do not put a smile on your face, then you will never be truly happy," said Itzak.

Tony thought about his words but couldn't agree. The simple things had never made him happy. He always needed more, bigger, better, faster. But events of the last twenty four hours were forcing him to reconsider all that.

Itzak wheeled around in his chair to look face to face at Amir.

"What is it my friend?" he asked. "What troubles you so?"

"Isn't it obvious?" said Amir with grunt. "You were right on the mark, Itzak, about our intentions and what Marija said about searching our hearts."

"Hey, I've been honest from the start!" said Tony. "And frankly, you'll be surprised to know, I'm really not the opportunistic scumbag you all seem to think I am." They all laughed. "Yes, I've been thinking about how we make money from this thing, whatever it is. But be honest, who wouldn't? If we don't, somebody else will. Is that such a sin?"

"No, you're right," said Amir. "And at least you have been honest about it. But Tony, you do have a tendency to relate everything anyone says to you and your experience. In this case, particularly, it seems like you have blinders on. You see only the money."

"I don't mean to sound condescending here but—you're young still. And let me tell you something about blinders; they help you stay focused. I don't live in a black and white world like you, my friend."

"What's that supposed to mean?" asked Amir.

"You know very well what it means, Amir. Tell me, is there such a thing as a good Serb? Hmm? Do you have any friends who are Serbs? Hmm? Black and white. I may be fixated on the money, but I'm honest and my conscience is clean as a whistle."

"But it's not money that's bothering you, is it?" asked Itzak. "Something else weighs on your conscience."

Amir stood looking out the window, he gave the impression he was debating whether or not to reveal his thoughts.

"Marija's message was confusing," he said, "that much I will agree…but the one thing that was crystal clear, I mean she must have said it like ten times, was this: only the *pure of heart* will understand the message."

"No," said Ivo, "what she said was that only the pure of heart will be *healed*."

"Either way," asked Itzak, "is your heart really in such need of purification?"

"Aren't all of ours?" said Ivo with a laugh.

Amir returned to the table and sat down. "Ivo, you're Catholic," he said, "let me ask you a question. Do you go to confession?"

"What?" said Ivo. "Well, sure, sometimes. Why?"

"I am fascinated by it. We don't have it in Islam. We don't accept the idea of a priest or clergy acting in God's place and granting absolution from sin. We regard Jesus as a great prophet but not as a divine being. Consequently, we reject the symbol of the cross and practice of Holy Communion and the act of Penance as well. I want to know, do you believe it really works?"

Ivo screwed up his face and hemmed and hawed. "Well, let's just say I'm counting on it! But seriously, if you are asking if I believe God is behind the curtain listening and that my sins are actually forgiven? Who knows? But I do know this much—I always feel better when I leave than when I went in."

"I think it's really the act of confessing more than the receiving of forgiveness that makes you feel better," said Tony. It's like what shrinks say: if you can name it, you can tame it."

"Well, for some reason, this whole business has had me obsessing on my faults, my sins," said Amir.

"Oh, well then Catholicism is perfect for you!" said Ivo.

Amir struggled to find the right words. "I want to hear the Lady's message! I want it to be true. But I don't think it's right to begin with lies. I need to explain my reason for going to Medjugorje."

"You don't have to," said Tony.

"I think I do," said Amir. "I ask only that you don't interrupt, as this is difficult enough." They all nodded and Amir finished his coffee. "I won't bother boring you with details that you all know so well, well except perhaps Tony. I'll try to be brief. I was born in Srebrenica and raised by my grandmother, because my father was a truck driver, like you Ivo, and always on the road delivering fruit and vegetables from down south. My mother worked in the light bulb factory on the assembly line."

"Forgive me, one interruption?" said Tony apologetically. "I keep seeing uncomfortable body language whenever the word Srebrenica is mentioned. What was…?"

"No, no, that's OK. I'm sorry, I just thought everyone knew. Srebrenica, my home town, was the site of the worst single massacre since the Holocaust. It was supposed to be a UN safe-haven, but that did little to stop the Serbs from killing thousands upon thousands in just a few days—right in front of the UN Peacekeepers. When the siege broke out and they rounded up all the men, I was only ten years old and my grandmother was able to hide me—at first. My father was on the road when it happened. I prayed that he would stay away and not come home, but there was no way to get word to him of what was happening."

"Did he eventually come home?" asked Itzak.

"I don't know. I never saw him again. It was not uncommon for men to disappear and never be heard from again. So, my mother went to the base camp of the Dutch peace-keepers to appeal to them for help. It took a long time. I waited and waited, peeking through the curtains but careful not to be seen. When I saw her coming up the hill towards our apartment, my heart leapt. She was just on the door step of the building when a Serb para-military called to her from across the street. She should have ignored him, but she didn't. She didn't, because she knew him. I went to school with his younger brother. We knew their family. His name was Radomir Glaven.

They spoke for a minute, first cordially, then more heated. Then he slapped her so hard she fell over. I almost cried out, but I didn't. She got to her knees and he grabbed her by the hair and dragger her across the street to a personnel carrier. Two other soldiers dragged her on board as she screamed. A minute later, she was gone forever. I didn't cry. But that night, I kissed my grandmother goodbye and I left. I crawled through the fields all the way to Zvornik. All night there were shots being fired on and around the road so I stayed clear of it. The escape was difficult but not impossible. Only once did I stop. In the darkness I could hardly see what was right in front of me and one time I fell into a ditch. I scrambled to climb out but the soil kept giving way around me. I felt trapped. I tried to run and jump up but I couldn't find my footing beneath me. A moment later, the moon appeared and I saw that the ditch I'd fallen into was actually a mass grave. I sat and I started to cry. I couldn't look at the faces. But instinctively, I knew that such a grave would not be uncovered for long. So, I piled several bodies against one side and managed to climb out. I said a prayer at the lip of the ditch for a moment then got moving. Eventually, I reached Zvornik and after a few days there, I headed for Tuzla."

He took out a handkerchief and blew his nose.

"Tony, the reason they don't call the Home in Tuzla an Orphanage is because so many of the children just don't know what happened to their parents. There are no death certificates for mass graves. Many of my brothers and sisters in the home were children of rape who had been abandoned. I was lucky compared to them."

"How do you figure?" asked Tony.

"Tell a child his parents have died, he will of course be sad and grieve. But in time, he will come to understand and move on. Tell a child that his parents abandoned him...and he has a lifetime of unanswered questions, guilt, self-doubt. I've seen a lot of it."

"And you never heard from either of your parents again?" asked Ivo.

"No. However, a few years ago, a group from America came to the home in Tuzla—probably the same group that Tony is part of. Their visit coincided with the tenth anniversary of the Srebrenica massacre. For the occasion, the UN was going to do a presentation, give speeches, the usual bullshit how we can never let this happen again. Then they all leave, feel better about themselves, and continue to do nothing. The same thing happened that day when the great hypocrite Bill Clinton came and opened the memorial. He acted as if the entire place was his doing, like he'd dug the graves, and planted the flowers. Ha! He did nothing for three years while tens of thousands died."

"Hey now," said Tony. "Let's be fair, he did end the conflict."

"Sure, and his wife dodged sniper fire in Sarajevo. Please! He was a coward. For three years the *New York Times* headlines are "Genocide in Bosnia" and all he would do was "consider options." Then, finally, a bread line in Sarajevo gets blown up live on CNN and he can't ignore it anymore but only because the rest of the world cries out: no more! Mr. Clinton fires a few cruise missiles into Serb positions in the hills around Sarajevo and they scatter like cockroaches; end of siege. Why did they wait three years to send those missiles? Why did their hand have to be forced?"

"Amir!" said Itzak firmly. "You were telling us about your parents?"

"Sorry." He cleared his throat and paused for a moment. "So, anyway, on this occasion, Germany did some more satellite imaging and discovered another mass grave. But after ten years, with no dental records and DNA testing still very expensive, identification seemed a dim prospect. But, as usual, the government said they 'would do what they could.'"

"And?" said Itzak.

"And I saw the names listed in the newspaper. Then, I packed a bag and went to visit my mother."

"She was..."

"Dead, of course. But that was to be expected. So, I went to the shiny new cemetery they constructed for the occasion, ironically, it lies directly across the street from the old sewing factory where thousands of Muslims were butchered. I found my mother's head stone and put a single white carnation on it, they were her favorite. She had simple tastes." He stood and began to pace around the room. "The plaque on the gates to the cemetery says, 'May revenge be turned into justice, may mothers' tears be turned into prayers that there should be no more Srebrenicas.'"

"Well, I guess at least you finally got some closure," said Tony.

"I guess. It's nice to have a place to go and visit my mom, occasionally bring a flower. But it doesn't change the fact that for ten years she laid rotting out in the woods somewhere. I have always blamed myself. I wondered if things would have been different if I hadn't been...such a coward."

"Oh Amir! You're not a coward! There was nothing you could do," they all protested.

Itzak stood and rubbed Amir's shoulders. Then the two men sat back down.

"And that's why you're going to Medjugorje?" said Tony.

Amir didn't answer. He just stared at the floor.

CHAPTER 14

SHAME AND MORE SHAME

Friday, 3:00am

When it became clear that Amir was not planning to say any more, Tony suspected that he'd asked the question too soon. After bearing his soul like that, the kid obviously needed a little down time with himself.

"Amir, if I may, I'd like to say one thing, and I hope you seriously consider my words," said Itzak. "I think it is very important at a time like this that you try hard not to confuse guilt with grief. They are not the same. You have every reason in the world to grieve, but you have nothing to feel guilty about."

"Every man is guilty of the good he chose not to do," said Amir.

"Not everyone is Voltaire, my friend, and not everyone is meant to be a hero. We act and react according to our gifts and everyone is blessed in different ways."

"Okay," said Tony, "I say we take a little break and get some air or coffee or something; this is getting a little bit heavy."

"Good idea," said Ivo, standing and stretching.

Amir stood up and went to the rest room.

Peter Danish

"That poor boy's had a life and half already," said Itzak.

"He sure has," said Tony. "Living through this nightmare isn't enough, some assholes have to throw guilt into the mess."

"It's very sad. That boy's guilt trails behind him like a shadow," said Itzak.

"Guilt is all in your head," said Ivo. "It never helps anybody. If anything, it makes us even more helpless than we already are."

"It may exist only in the mind, but that won't prevent it from ruining your life and torturing your soul," said Tony.

A troubling thought came to him, and he immediately resolved to fix it.

"OK, Ivo, look, while Amir's in the can we need to speak plainly, and fast. That kid isn't going along with any plan we come up with if he doesn't completely trust us."

"I agree," said Ivo, nodding.

"So, we all need a big favor from you, pal. I know you are a very private person, but you're the only one here that Amir likes and trusts. When he comes out, you must tell him why you're going to Medjugorje. Everything rests on it. I don't care if you have to make something up."

"I thought the whole point was to be honest," said Ivo.

"He does have a point," said Itzak.

"Look, Ivo, you're right!" said Tony. "You're 100% right. But we have no time to debate. We can all laugh about it later, but right now, Amir has opened up to us and he's hurting. We can't offer him absolution but we can show him empathy. You're closest to him. Now, when he comes out, I want you to let him know he's not alone."

"I assume that means…"

Just then Amir came out and returned to the table. They all went silent.

"No, no. Don't stop on my account," said Amir. "Besides, I have a question." He looked squarely at Tony. "Now that I am a full-fledged associate Hollywood producer, I want to know who I am working for. One thing has been bothering me about your story; you never even mentioned Medjugorje when you told us about your movie. So, what part does it play in your script? Did the runaway bride and the American tourist stop in Medjugorje on their way to their new life in Italy?"

Tony laughed out loud, hoping to lighten the mood, but he saw it wasn't really working.

"Well, um, I, ah." He stumbled for words as his mind raced. He wasn't sure he was quite ready to share with these people on that level yet. He looked at Amir and saw the pain in his face and realized that he'd have to come clean pretty soon. Why not now?

"Well, I wish I had a more colorful story to tell. Maybe that's why I make movies? Anyway, I guess there's a little bit more to my story but not all that much and it's kind of personal but, um, well, what the hell, since we're bearing souls…" He looked at Itzak and thought, this guy is fighting cancer and he's here looking for a miracle. He wasn't ashamed to admit it. Why should *I*?

"You know what, fuck it. The real reason I came to Bosnia—the first time—that's right, the first time; I have actually been here once before. And the first time I came was a couple of years ago. My wife and I, we were, we had, um, been trying to start a family. For quite a while actually and …well let's just say, things weren't turning out as we planned. Then, one day, a buddy of mine in New York was showing me pictures of his trip to Tuzla with this human rights organization. He showed me pictures of the most beautiful bunch of children I'd ever seen. It was an eye-opener for me because he told me they were all Muslim. It might sound really stupid to you but, in all honesty, I had never seen or frankly even considered, a blonde-haired, blue-eyed Muslim before! They weren't all blonde, of course, but that thought stuck with me; just how far off so many of my preconceptions were."

He swirled around the wine in his glass for a minute as he tried to compose himself.

"Something inside me changed that day. For reasons I can't explain, I wanted more than anything to visit the home."

"And?" asked Amir.

"And…I did. And it was incredible. I mean, these kids…you see…they were playing soccer on the concrete of the street. Their shoes were falling apart and their little feet were bleeding, yet they were so friggin' joyful."

He began to tear up. He really didn't want to lose it, but there was little he could do.

"They were more than beautiful, they were perfect. And they didn't have a goddamn pot to piss in. They were so happy to see us. And so grateful for even the slightest gesture of human kindness. The realization that I was in a position to give, that I was capable of bringing so much happiness, so easily, to so many. Well, I can't describe it. It was like crack. I just wanted more!"

He wiped away a tear.

"So, when I got home, I called my buddy again and I asked

him if the home allowed adoption from the US. He didn't know. So, my wife and I tried to reach the home through the consulate and that proved a complete waste of time. So, we flew here again and visited the kids at the home and tried directly through the Bosnian government. But they are either completely incompetent or completely corrupt, I don't know which. Or maybe both. Either way... it never happened."

He stood up and walked over to the window.

"My wife and I are separated now, and I desperately want to reconcile, but truth is, I really, really wanted to see the kids again. So, when I came here to research the film, I made a side trip to Tuzla. Unfortunately, when I got there, they informed me that the laws had changed since I was here last and we were now too old to adopt!"

Silence filled the room.

"But as always, if I could come up with a good reason for them to make an exception in my case, they would consider it. I'm not a rich man. So, that door closed on me as well."

"But, while planning the trip, I heard about Medjugorje, and when I saw that my route was taking me so close by, I decided to visit it for myself and to pray for a little miracle in my own life. So, I applied and got some grant money together to come over here to research a film. I was thinking of a low budget documentary at first, that was true. Then an indie, you know, art house, but something that would turn a profit and at least help me get back on my feet financially. But God, ever since meeting Marija, hell, I'm thinking major budget feature."

"So, you really are researching this film?" said Ivo.

"Yes! Yes, of course. My life has been a total mess lately, but I thought through this film, I could turn my mess into my message. A message that in spite of all, there's always time to change and always time for second chance. But I got completely sidetracked when I met Marija, and heard about the secrets. Shit, I bet I could get Spielberg to direct it now!"

"Pft!" said Amir with disgust.

"No, really," said Tony. "I actually know him a little from way back."

"I'm sure you do," said Amir. "But, trust me, he doesn't care about Bosnia."

"But, you said it yourself, this could change history!"

"In 1994, your Mr. Steven Spielberg had a chance to change history and he chose not to," said Amir.

Tony scanned around in confusion; he saw he was not alone.

"Sorry, I guess I need to brush up on my Spielberg history."

"In March of that year, we were living in a basement, huddled around a tiny television watching...hoping...praying, that with the whole world watching, Mr. Spielberg would win the Oscar for "Schindler's List." For if he did, he would surely say something about the people suffering in Bosnia. For God's sake, his movie was about genocide! How could he not?" He paused and relaxed. "Well, he did win. But he did not mention Bosnia. Maybe his good friend Bill Clinton asked him not to. He did say the usual, 'We can never let this happen again!' But sadly, I think he meant, we can never left this happen to Jews again. If he had said, 'People, as we speak tonight, terrible atrocities are happening to our brothers and sisters in Bosnia and it must be stopped!' over a billion people world-wide would have heard him, and I believe in my heart, Srebrenica might never have happened."

The room was silent. The idea sank in. Tony was depressed. He decided to try to lighten the mood just a bit.

"Okay, how about George Lucas? Kidding. Just kidding."

Ivo slammed his fist on the table. "God damn it! You're never serious! Everything is a fucking joke to you! Ever think maybe your jokes are disrespectful?"

"Come on, Ivo! You know I was just trying to…"

"It doesn't matter! You make a fucking joke of everything. This is not some American talk show! People here don't enjoy looking like fools! I don't want to tell you anything because I am positive you will only make a joke of it!"

They sat in silence again for a minute. Tony realized he botched the situation again. He made a quick decision: no more attempts at humor with these folks; they either don't get it or they don't want to get it. Either way, he was consistently getting undesired results.

"You're right," he said softly and slowly. "I admit I can be pretty thoughtless sometimes and I always try to put a happy face on everything, I can't help it, it's just my nature." He looked directly at Ivo. "Anyway, I'm sorry, Ivo. *Oprostite.*"

The Croat struggled and for a moment Tony wasn't sure his olive branch would be well received.

"You should just say: *Oprosti,*" said Ivo. "I accept your apology, because I see now just how hard it is for you not to be a jerk all the time, it doesn't come natural."

"Gee, thanks," said Tony.

"And forgive me, because my English is not so great and maybe I am not always choosing the right word."

"No problem. Your English is just fine."

"You know, maybe you don't realize, but I have spoken more English in last twenty four hours than in my entire life! I do this out of respect for fact that you don't speak Croatian and it is a lot of work, okay?"

Tony smiled at the thought, because Ivo was actually correct, it had not dawned on him.

"I have tried to not dislike you but we...we are just so different. To say we live in different worlds is not enough. And me, I just don't like talking about personal things, you know. I like to keep to myself."

"Then don't," said Itzak. "No one is forcing you."

"Tell them what you told me about Medjugorje, Ivo," said Amir.

"I just wanted to see site of the Virgin, make confession," said Ivo shaking his head. "No big deal. It's just... well...you see, I never believe in miracles... and I honestly don't know if the children really see the Blessed Virgin or not... but I do know one thing about Medjugorje, and that is, during the war...over 4,000 Serb bombs fell on Medjugorje. Over 4000! And the only casualties were one cow, two chickens, and one dog. And *that* my friends, is a miracle."

The implications of his words left them all speechless.

"Wow. That's amazing! I didn't know that," said Tony.

"Look, Ivo," said Amir, "if you feel uncomfortable..."

Ivo chuckled to himself. "No, you are right. You are totally right. Marija deserves honesty. If she is going to break a great confidence for us, we should at least have good intentions. Catholic guilt, you know!"

He lit another cigarette.

"Is it wrong that nearly twenty years later, the war still is all we talk about? It's like we had no lives before and have no lives after."

"It is completely understandable," said Itzak, "and also quite common."

"Anyway, for me, the war didn't start in 91, like history books say. Real war began in 1990, when Dinamo Zagreb ultras, played football match against Red Star Belgrade. Football is religion to most Croats. So, when Red Star came to Zagreb for league title game it was really big deal. Five thousand fans come along with them, all wearing their stupid red jerseys—you couldn't miss them! Before game, there were fights in streets. Everyone knew there would be trouble. The game never even got started. Serb fans began to chant stupid nationalist things like 'Zagreb is Serbian' and 'We'll kill Tudjman!'"

"Tudjman?" asked Tony.

"Croatian President," said Amir.

"Got it."

"Anyway, Croats start chanting back at them. Then, Serbs begin to rip out seats and throw them all on field. So, Croats in upper deck start dumping beer down on Serbs. So, police step in to break it up. But of course police are all Serbian Yugoslav police, so they only beat up Croats. Finally, Red Star fans break down fence and come out onto field and complete chaos breaks out. Serb fans with knives stab many Croat fans and ugly riot starts. Next thing you know, armored vehicles with big water cannons arrive…and you just knew people were going to die."

"Ivo, sorry to interrupt, but what exactly does it have to do with Medjugorje?" asked Tony gingerly.

"Oh, sorry, I almost forgot. You see, most of Dinamo's fans enlisted in Croatian Army when war started and of course, Serb rivals joined Serb army. Each time my unit captured a Serb soldier, I would ask him if he was at Maksimir stadium for Dinamo-Red Star match. If he said yes, we would kill him."

"And if he said no?" asked Amir.

"Please!" said Ivo. "We were not savages!"

Tony's blood ran cold.

"Hey, Ivo," said Tony. "Um, you…you do know I was just kidding about the mouthwash and the deodorant right?"

"Do you want to hear the rest?" said Ivo.

"There's more?" said Tony, terrified to hear anymore.

"Not really, I guess. Just more of the same. Sorry it's not noble or important like…"

"No, no! That's fine. The whole idea is for it to help you."

"Help me. Ha! In '91, I ask my girlfriend Marija to marry me."

"Tell me something," said Tony, "is every woman in this entire country named Maria?"

"Just about. Most. Maybe half," they responded together.

"Anyway, we were both at Maksimir Stadium on day when riot happen. On day when Boban became national hero for standing up to police. Marija beg me not to get into fight, but when I saw my friends, well…so, I tell her to stay in her seat. I go onto field. I didn't get arrested, but I was part of group chased off by soldiers. We were forced out onto street while fighting inside got worse. I try to go back in to find Marija but I could not. So, I walk to her house and wait for her to come home. But she never come home. I wait all night. Finally hospital calls. She is in intensive care unit. A bottle hit her in her face at stadium. She was cut badly and lost a lot of blood. But she was alright and out of danger." He paused and grit his teeth and flared his nostrils like an animal. "She lost sight in left eye and had big…big scar on cheek down to her mouth."

He stood up and walked to the bar.

"You think the liquor closet is open?" he said. "I could really use a drink."

"I saw a jug of wine on the floor next to the fridge," said Tony.

Ivo brought the jug back to the table. He swigged his coffee and poured wine into the coffee cup. He took a deep drink.

"Marija wanted to call off our wedding, but I wouldn't let her. She say that if I marry her now…I marry her out of pity, out of…. obligation. Well, we married. It didn't work out. She left me after only one year. She told me it would have been better if she died. She never understood, it didn't matter to me what she look like. I love her. She says to me: *is too hard to live with nothing to live for.*"

He filled the cup again and drained it slowly.

"Maybe a month later…she drank some stove cleaning liquid. She died three days later from internal bleeding."

He filled his cup yet again and Itzak stood up and rubbed his shoulders.

Tony was emotionally wiped out and he felt like crying. He struggled to keep it together and to remain focused, but it wasn't working.

"Whew. OK, let's take five," he said.

Ivo got up and headed for the rest rooms.

"Jesus Christ," said Tony. "This stuff is just so far from my world. Honest to God, I don't know how you people get up every day."

"Getting soft on us?" said Amir. "Okay, while Ivo is in the bathroom, let's try to re-focus."

Tony was surprised to hear the young man speaking in such a business-like fashion, but also glad to hear it. Someone else was starting to move the plan forward and it helped motivate him.

"Alright," said Tony. "Let's speak frankly for just a minute and I promise most sincerely that this is the last time I'm going to be the 'Ugly American,' okay? But we all realize now that if this message Marija's writing down actually contains something, some kind of...I don't know, some means to heal or cure disease, well, we are looking at the motherlode here. And I hope it does, if for no other reason than to give some solace to all of you folks."

Ivo returned from the men's room.

"The *Holy-Mother*-load?" he said.

"Sorry, Ivo," said Tony, "I didn't see you. But let's be serious for a sec. We might want to put something in writing sooner rather than later just to make sure we all, you know, respect each other's claim to a share."

"I still find it somewhat obscene to talk about profiting from a holy message like it's a commodity," said Amir.

"Wait, wait, wait!" said Itzak. "Let me speak for a second because I believe I may be the only one of us with a vested interest other than an economic one here. I can say without reservation...if this message is indeed genuine and can do as Marija has suggested, I gladly relinquish any claim to any profits derived from it."

"That's very honorable of you, Itzak," said Ivo.

"But, you won't need to. Because we are not sharing it equally," said Amir.

"What do you mean?" said Tony.

"Perhaps I did not make myself perfectly clear," said Amir. "I mean that I would rather die than share this knowledge with a Serb—especially that one."

"Whoa!" said Tony. "Now hang on, we agreed…"

"Yes, we agreed to work together and not to argue or fight, fine! We did not agree to share the profits from the discovery equally. And I will not. Period."

After a moment of stony silence and contemplation, Ivo nodded. He was siding with Amir.

"I agree. Come on, Tony! The guy's an asshole. You said it yourself!"

"I don't care! We made a deal."

"You have no idea what these people are like, what they are capable of. They're the lowest creatures on earth," said Amir.

"Hello? I'm from Hollywood?" said Tony. "I know a little bit about slimy creatures. But look, I don't like the guy either, but we made an agreement. And my word is my bond."

They sat and simmered in the dark for a several minutes.

"What if the Serb should break the agreement?" asked Itzak. "Then would you agree to cut him out?"

Tony was frightened by Itzak's tone of voice. He really didn't like the sound of this, but he was also keenly aware that he was a foreigner in a foreign place and they could just as easily cut him out and he'd have very little recourse.

"He's a fucking atheist anyway!" said Ivo. "You heard him; he called it all bullshit!"

"Exactly!" said Amir. "And I for one do not care for an infidel cashing in on a miraculous gift!"

"Look, first of all, we don't know he's an atheist," said Tony.

"They're all atheists, communists!" said Ivo. "They only roll out the crosses when it benefits them. They have no real faith."

"Alright already! Enough!" said Tony. "If you can prove he's an atheist or that he's violated our agreement, then we cut him out. Otherwise, he's still our partner, clear?"

"Done! Now, how do we do it?" asked Ivo.

"Don't worry," said Amir. "He'll do it for us. He can't help himself."

"Okay, then!" said Tony. "Let's call it a night and at least try to get some shut eye. We're gonna need clear heads tomorrow."

He stood and gathered up the coffee cups and put them on the counter.

"I'm think I'm going to have one more cigarette," said Itzak.

"I'll join you," said Amir.

"Suit yourselves," said Tony. "Let's go, Ivo."

They walked through the darkness to the stairs and ascended them.

CHAPTER 15

GODS, GUNS, AND GREED

Friday, 3:30am

Tony dropped onto the bed with a thud. For the first time in ages, he felt really hopeful. These guys were from another world but they were starting to feel like friends. Claire would be proud of him, he thought, and the thought made him smile.

Claire deserved to feel proud of him, to feel she'd made the right choice. She had handled the ups and downs like a seasoned sailor, and had precious little good fortune as a result. But she always managed to stay positive and stay beautiful. Her light radiated positive energy and it fueled Tony and gave him the strength to carry on every day.

However, eventually even she had her limit. Unfortunately, Tony was a bad judge of when to push and when to hold back. He always enjoyed the company of young actresses. He sold himself as the sage veteran filmmaker who could guide their careers, telling himself that it kept him young. He caught himself thinking that he was about to do it again with Marija. Many of the actresses believed him and were anxious to show their gratitude, which he uniformly turned away. He loved the attention and he was a world class flirt, but since he'd met Claire, he was a one woman man. What he never realized was just how hurt and how jealous Claire might be even if she never gave him a hint of it. She trusted him 99.9% but she didn't trust the young girls around him at all, and she wished, secretly, that he would just stop putting himself in situations where something might happen. Nothing ever did—nothing really. But that tiny little sneaking suspicion on her part did more damage to their relationship than either had ever realized.

He rolled over onto his back and stared at the ceiling. He debated and toyed with the idea of saying a prayer. It had been quite a while since he felt that way. He remembered what his father had told him as a child: 'Don't bother praying when it rains if you don't pray when the sun shines.' Turned out his father was quoting the great pitcher Satchel Page. As a kid, it held no meaning to him, but as he lay there, it haunted him. He thought praying now would make him feel like a hypocrite. Well…he'd been called a lot worse. So, at the risk of feeling like a hypocrite, he folded his hands together and said a quiet prayer.

In his heart he knew it was a selfish prayer but he did it just the same, he did it for Claire. Feeling hypocritical was a small price to pay to have her back.

Whatever the next twenty-four hours might hold, he knew one thing: he was a changed man, changed for good.

"Ah, Christ! Now I'm quoting goddamn Broadway tunes."

He punched the pillow into shape and buried his face in it. Two deep sighs later, he was sound asleep.

Amir let out a great yawn and stretched his tired arms.

"Want some more coffee?" asked Itzak.

"Please," he said.

Itzak got up and got the coffee pot from the counter and poured two cups for them. Then, he replaced the pot on the burner and rejoined Amir at the table. His demeanor had changed. It made Amir feel a bit uneasy. He walked over to the window. He opened it and looked out into the night air.

"The rain has stopped," he said. He shut the window and walked back to the table.

"Feel like a little fresh air?"

"Sure," said Amir.

They grabbed their cups and stepped outside into the gravel parking lot in front of the rest stop. The clouds were beginning to part and pale blue moonlight lit the trees. They stood there smoking for a moment or two before Itzak spoke up.

"So, tell me," asked Itzak with a frosty smile, "why exactly would a Muslim ask the Blessed Virgin of the Catholic Church for forgiveness for anything?"

"What?" asked Amir.

Itzak smiled and laughed to himself gently.

"Ah, you may have fooled them but you cannot pull the wool over Itzak's eyes. You're not here for forgiveness for anything, are you?"

Amir was perspiring and tapping his foot. He dragged deeply on his cigarette.

"I wasn't when I left Sarajevo. But I am now."

"What does that mean? And why are you sweating?"

Amir wiped his forehead with his sleeve; he was perspiring like crazy. He took a deep breath. It was clear he was debating whether or not to share any more. He looked up at a cloud passing in front of the moon. It cast them both back into darkness.

"This is not my first visit to Medjugorje," he said.

"So?" said Itzak.

"Last year I visited Mostar with my school. After the long bus ride from Sarajevo, I was exhausted, so I went straight to the hotel to go to bed. But as I was checking in, I signed the hotel log book. And there it was, a few lines above my name, two simple words: Radomir Glaven."

"Good Lord!"

"Yes, Good Lord, indeed. Well, my heart began to race and my head was spinning. Was it him? How could I tell? What room was he in? How could I find out? But, as fate would have it, the elevator opened and out he stepped... with his wife and his little boy. Fourteen years and a few gray hairs later, but it was him."

"What did you do?"

"Nothing."

"Nothing?"

"Nothing—*yet*. But, I will. I will kill him. And now that I knew where he lived, I could take my time. Plan."

"But how did you find out where he lived?"

"The desk clerk was Bosnian."

"Of course," said Itzak. "And let me guess, Glaven lives in Medjugorje?"

Amir nodded.

"So much for the pure of heart."

"My conscience is clean," said Amir.

"For the moment, but your heart is blackening rapidly," said Itzak. He lit another cigarette and shook his head in disgust. "Amir, there's always a reason for violence, but rarely a good one. Revenge is very costly business. I thought you were a student? Wanted to go to America? Was that all a lie?"

"No! Not at all! I do want to study and to go to America, but, I never imagined I'd have the opportunity to avenge my mother. Surely, it is what Allah intended?"

Itzak shook his head. "I don't know. I am no longer a religious man, but I am a reasonable one and I can tell you that you will be throwing your life away if you kill him."

"The Qur'an says, 'If anyone kills a man deliberately, he is to be handed over to the relatives of the one who has been killed. If they wish, they may kill him.'" He paused and looked down at his hands, balled into fists. "I wanted blood...but then, tonight, listening to Marija, hearing her beautiful words, I was griped with tremendous conflict."

"Amir, Islam does not teach Muslims to seek revenge on *anyone*. Rather, Islam commands Muslims to repel evil with good deeds and to forgive and forget. My friend, we can do this all night! In the Quran, like most scripture, if you look hard enough, you can always find a quotation to support almost any argument!"

"I admire your knowledge, Itzak. Tell me, why did you stop being a rabbi? What would make a man like you do something like that?"

Itzak laughed.

"Strictly speaking, once you are a rabbi, you are a rabbi for life. But, I did leave my congregation. I'd love to say, 'it's a very tough question and complicated answer,' but it really was not. Did you know, the word 'rabbi' actually comes from the Hebrew word *rav*, which in biblical Hebrew means 'great' or 'revered.' But in general terms, 'a religious teacher.'" Amir shook his head. "When I felt I was no longer capable of teaching, had nothing left to give, I felt I could no longer be a rabbi. Simple."

"But you're a wonderful teacher! You've taught me so much in just a few hours!"

"Because you, my friend, are a seeker... but your numbers are dwindling. I have a confession to make that I believe you already have started to suspect."

"You're not from Slovenia?"

"I am. But haven't been for some time. We left for America after World War II, I was just a boy. The Shoah devastated Slovenia and there was nothing left for us. I have taught at a Yeshiva in New York for many years. But no more."

"But why?"

"I believe that if you brought together all of the liars, thieves, cheats, back-stabbers, all of the evil doers in the entire world and eliminated them in one grand sweep, the world would not change one bit. In no time at all they would all reappear. Just in different visage, with different names."

"You mean the devil?"

"Oh Amir, please! You know better. There is no devil. He is a man-made creation, and I believe he was made in man's own savage and ugly image. No, I mean mankind! As a species! Good, bad, black, white, gay, straight, what difference does any of it make when forever the exact same pattern always emerges. Society can't help but pour, but heap success and riches on the strong and the ambitious and the ruthless and the violent and the evil. Now, even laws are irrelevant. This is why moral law is the only law that matters! Morality must be like physics, like geometry; unalterable...not open to interpretation."

"I thought you said this was a simple answer?"

The sound of an owl caught their attention and caused Amir to jump. Itzak couldn't help but laugh.

"Careful! You heard the old man! The devil lurks in these woods!"

"Very funny," said an embarrassed Amir.

Itzak took a long deep breath of the night air and very slowly released it. It seemed he was drinking in the night itself.

"Amir, Judaism considers 'Tikkun Olam,' or the 'perfecting the world,' as the fundamental reason for God's creating the world in the first place. But we are such a disappointment on virtually every level. According to our faith, we are born morally pure—not like the poor Catholics burdened with original sin. But then what? The cycle begins again. Every man from ten thousand years ago to today is on that same slope, sliding down to moral mediocrity or worse. Is our world perfecting? Is it one iota better than it was a thousand years ago?"

"Did something in particular trigger this excruciating level of self-examination?" asked Amir.

Itzak laughed and slapped Amir on the back.

"Very good! You should be a psychologist my friend, not a historian. Of course something triggered it! Two very simple words. I will whisper them to you so listen closely: Bernie Madoff."

"Bernie Madoff?"

"You know of him?"

"I think so," said Amir. The American who stole all the people's money?"

"That is one way of putting it."

"Is there another?"

"Yes, Amir. There is. He stole something far more important than money. He stole their trust. He stole their faith. He stole two of God's greatest gifts. He has done so much more than take people's financial security, he has ruined them, heart and soul, forever. Thousands and thousands and thousands of people. The old, the sick! And he did it with two very simple words: trust me."

"And because he was Jewish you lost your faith?"

"No. But because he was a Jew, so many blindly put their faith in him! People like me. What they believed was the greatest trust, was in fact, the greatest betrayal. Worst of all...I personally counseled my congregation to trust him, to invest with him. Widows who came to me for advice with their life savings...I told them: Trust me! He will not let you down. Then I watched so many, colleagues, friends, neighbors... In my mind, if you tell someone 'trust me' and then lie to them, your sin is not doubled, it is ten-fold. For me Amir, it was like the 'fall of man' all over again."

"But the sin is his, not yours! You didn't lie. You didn't force them to invest!"

"Well, not exactly," said Itzak with a hint of nervous laughter. "After all, my personal investment had paid incredible dividends, you see. As treasurer, I had access to the congregation's accounts. I only did what I thought was in everyone's best interest."

"Oh, Itzak!" said Amir. Then an unthinkable thought crossed his mind. "Wait, a second...are you on the run from the law?"

"It was just a matter of time before it was discovered, so I fled."

Just then they heard a creak at the window and they turned around, but saw nothing.

"The wind," said Itzak.

"Wow. And your religion, your faith?"

Itzak took another deep sip of coffee.

"Judaism is a beautiful, beautiful religion, Amir. I no longer felt worthy of it. My depression was profound and painful. But I ignored the pain for too long. And then, as if one great elaborate joke was being played on me..."

"Cancer."

Itzak nodded, looked at his cigarette, the tossed it away and started back toward the door. Amir followed silently. But just as they reached the door, Itzak motioned to Amir to stop and stay quiet. He leaned forward and stealthily gazed in through the window. A tiny red light was glowing inside. Itzak gasped and beckoned for Amir to join him at the window.

Inside the rest stop, they could see Marija dressed in her stark white night dress. She was kneeling on the floor in front of the little statue of the Madonna and praying. She was lost in reverence and looked positively radiant in the soft glowing candle light. She had beads in her hands which Itzak recognized as rosary beads. She kneeled there, still as a statue, for a long time.

Amir was amazed at her self-control and her poise. He had not taken a close look at the statue all day and now as he inspected it in the candlelight, he was not impressed. The paint was peeling off and decades of cigarette smoke had faded the colors from blues and pinks to grays and browns. He also noticed that one of the Madonna's hands had actually broken off, and that a rather large spider web connected her veil to the window sill next to it.

Yet, when Marija gazed upon her namesake, she saw none of it. She didn't see the peeling paint, the faded colors or the spider web. To her, it was the most beautiful, most sacred vision she'd ever seen. She stared at the little statue as if it were the Virgin Mary herself.

After about twenty minutes, she came out of her spell. She made the sign of the cross and stood up. She gently put out the candle and slowly ascended the stairs.

Itzak and Amir were at the window, speechless. Itzak had tears in his eyes; clearly the scene had struck a sensitive spot in his soul. He quietly opened the door and went back inside. Once inside, he walked to the counter and picked up the other coffee cups there. He walked behind the counter and placed the cups in the sink and ran the water to rinse them.

Amir was silent and at a loss for words. He wandered over to the Madonna and looked at the spot where Marija had held her vigil.

"Perhaps our Serbian friend has the advantage on us after all," said Itzak.

"In what way?"

Itzak turned off the water and wiped his hands with a towel.

"If you never had faith, you can never know the pain and the emptiness of losing it."

Itzak was in pain, pain from a wound that showed no visible scars. Amir desperately wanted to help him.

"You don't sound to me like a man who's lost his faith," said Amir. "You chose to step aside during your time of crisis, rather than pollute your brothers with hate; to me that sounds like a man of high principles."

"If only it were that simple. Leading them to ruin, then abandoning them in their time of need?"

"Itzak, only an hour ago, you told me that Islam commands us to forgive our enemies and yet you are not capable of forgiving even yourself."

Itzak came out from behind the counter and leaned on the bar. His face wore a sad smile. "My dear, Amir, forgiving ourselves is always the hardest."

"Only for good men!" exclaimed Amir. "And I think you are a good man, Itzak. Let me put to you the same question you asked me: are you coming to Medjugorie seeking a cure? Or seeking forgiveness?"

Itzak pursed his lips and though for a moment.

"I come seeking…time. I have many many sins on my conscience and I need time to atone for them. I'm not yet ready to face my friends again, let alone my maker."

"Do you believe in miracles?" asked Amir without the slightest hint of sarcasm or levity.

"You want to know what I think is a real miracle? Faith. That anyone can have faith in anything or anyone anymore. I miss having it, I long to regain it, but I'm afraid I've just become too skeptical. God, the very idea of God, requires a leap of faith now. And I was once cement-firm in my belief and my convictions, but life and living in our time has shattered them."

Amir listened in silence, fearing an interruption might cause Itzak to shut down again. He simply looked at his coffee cup and didn't raise his eyes.

"But, I'll tell you something very funny and quite ironic. I have recently felt a spark of faith in the deepest recesses of my heart that I have not known in quite a long time, and it was born in the strangest of ways. I was in Fatima earlier this summer and I visited the holy shrine there. I was immediately struck by the wonderful warmth of the people there, genuinely lovely, caring people. But I also saw crass commercialism at its absolute worst, third-rate phony charlatans selling false hope to the sick, and it caused my heart to harden again. What beasts these people were!"

"I sat on the ground and took my shoes off near the mount where the children saw the Blessed Virgin. I looked up to the heavens with anger. I was angry at God for allowing it. Then I thought to myself, 'well this is quite the conundrum!' I'd found myself angry and cursing someone that I didn't believe existed; whom I had firmly decided was the creation of man. It gave me pause. But it also caused me to wonder. It made me seriously wonder how a creature as base and despicable as man could possibly be capable of conceiving a concept as beautiful and perfect as a loving God! Did I believe it was really possible? The answer was 'no.' I did not believe it possible that man was capable of such a wondrous creation. And therein lies the irony. I began to reconsider the existence of God…because I could not believe man capable of creating Him!"

Amir looked up at Itzak and smiled.

"There are many roads!" he said with a laugh. "And this one has brought you to Medjugorje."

"Quite true! You know, while I was in Lourdes recently I did a bit of reading about this place."

Lourdes, Fatima, thought Amir, *he isn't leaving any stone unturned is he?* The apparent contradiction that Itzak was able to consider the miraculous at a time when his belief in God was shaky at best made Amir smile inwardly. He was beginning to feel real affection for the old man.

"After reading about Medjugorje, in truth, I was not very convinced. But then I read an interesting statistic. Did you know that a recent survey showed that world-wide, 99% of doctors believe that religious faith can heal a sick patient? Doctors! Not priests, imams, or rabbis—doctors! Then I came across the account of an Italian doctor who had come to study the children during the visions. It impressed me deeply. He literally hooked them to electrocardiogram and electro-encephalograms and monitored their heart and brain functions during the actual visions."

"Wow. What did he learn?"

"He learned virtually nothing. They registered almost no perceptible differences during the visions. However, he did notice something else, not about the children, but an incredible phenomenon. Each time, just at the moment that the children's visions began... all birds in the trees went completely silent. And *that*, my friend, is why I'm going to Medjugorje."

He stretched and yawned, then he stood up from the counter and headed slowly for the stairs.

"Amir, I've greatly enjoyed talking with you, but let's get some rest now. I don't want to oversleep and miss breakfast. After all, it's never a good idea to change the course of human history on an empty stomach."

Amir rushed over to Itzak and gave him a hug. The old man accepted it warmly.

"You coming to bed?"

"I'm coming," said Amir. "I'll just turn off the stove first."

"*Laku noc*, Amir."

"*Laku noc.*"

Itzak disappeared upstairs as Amir picked up his cigarettes from the table. He paused then walked over and looked at the statue of the Virgin Mary. It looked cheap to him, hardly a worthy representation of the Mother of God. But its power on a true believer like Marija was undeniable. It gave him chills to look at it, like it had some kind of…curse on it. He picked up his coffee cup and walked behind the counter. He paused for a moment and after fiddling with something under the counter, he headed for the stairs.

He stopped at the bottom thinking he'd heard something. He looked around in the darkness. It was the rain; it had started once again. Once he identified it, the sound relaxed him. He strode up the stairs and went to his room hoping he'd be able to get some rest.

The café was silent and completely dark. Only the sound of the rain on the glass disturbed the perfect night. The air was still foggy from the smoke of countless cigarettes.

Suddenly, from the hallway leading to the restrooms, the sound of a match being struck could be heard. The match flame lit a cigarette and the cigarette glowed in the darkness. A figure was leaning against the wall in the darkness. Then, stealthily, it stepped forward out of the hall and into the dining area and into the moonlight. The silhouetted figure walked over to the table that the men had been sitting at and he nodded his head.

"My friends," he said under his breath. As he said it, he lifted his head up and allowed the moonlight to illuminate his features. It was the Serb.

After a moment, he walked behind the counter. He reached under the counter and pulled out the old man's shot gun. He tucked the gun under his arm while he took one last drag from his cigarette.

Then he threw the cigarette in the sink. He came out from behind the counter and slowly walked up the stairs with the gun over his shoulder.

CHAPTER 16

MORNING IN MEDJUGORJE

Friday, 9:30am

The sunlight streaming in from the window reached Tony's eyes and awakened him. He had no clue of the time but he thought, what a wonderful alarm clock! This must have been how primitive man woke up. He felt a bit like primitive man this morning. He was facing a day that quite possibly would change the course of his life. He knew he was ready to face it but he was still uncertain about his companions; their silly religious zealousness might get in the way of his plans.

He could tell that the bleakness of their world view was more than simply PTSD. It was the *sturm und drang* of their daily lives every day since the end of the war, living with the ghosts.

He hated thinking of himself as a callous opportunist but that was the way they'd all painted him and hearing it repeatedly gave him pause. Could they be right? Even on some level? In the natural course of events, he wouldn't have cared one bit what they thought, but there was something different this time, and he knew what it was. It was Marija. She was the wild card in all this. For some reason that he could not put his finger on, he didn't want her to think poorly of him.

What would she think of them cutting the Serb out of the deal? Even if he had it coming. Did he have it coming? The Serb was a real puzzle to Tony, much more than any of the others—with the possible exception of Itzak. The real tragedy was that the Serb wasn't just another dullard who had been morally and emotionally ravaged by the war. If he had been, in all likelihood he would simply have given his life over to alcohol and died in the gutter like all the others. No, he was clearly a bright guy, well-educated, and the horror show of his recent past was allowing him no peace. Tony didn't like him, that much was certain, but he also couldn't hate him.

Tony rolled over and saw that Itzak was already up, so he didn't need to be quiet. He put on his shoes and headed for the bathroom in the hall. When he opened the door, he saw Itzak and Amir chatting away at the top of the stairs. He would have said good morning but his mind was fixed on the thought of a hot shower.

Itzak and Amir were sharing a laugh as they descended the stairs when a strange image met their gaze.

Downstairs in the dining room, the Serb was behind the counter humming to himself as he shoveled eggs from a frying pan onto a plate! They couldn't believe their eyes. They just looked at each other and shrugged.

"What time is it?" Itzak asked.

"It's past ten already," answered the Serb. "*Dobro jutro!*"

"*Jutro,*" said Itzak. "Why are you cooking? The old man hired you?"

"No, but he did leave me in charge, so to speak," said the Serb. "He made fresh bread and coffee for everyone. I found some eggs and thought there'd be no harm."

"Where is he?"

"He needed to run into town to buy provisions. I told him to go ahead, we'd be fine."

"He wasn't afraid to leave his daughter alone with Tony?" said Amir.

"He seemed more worried about us trying to skip out on the bill."

"Of course he was," said Itzak.

"But, I told him, we had nowhere to go until the bus came and that won't be for hours. So, it's just us for a while."

"What kind of eggs?" asked Amir.

"Only scrambled, I'm afraid. I'm frying some for myself."

"Did you say something about coffee?"

"Help yourself!" said the Serb with a grin.

Amir looked at the Serb suspiciously.

"Thanks."

"Well, I must say, you seem awfully bright and positive this morning," said Itzak.

"I find a good night's sleep often helps put things in perspective, don't you?" said the Serb with a big smile.

"I do. But, I am glad to hear you say it," said Itzak.

"Go on, eat while it's still hot."

Amir and Itzak didn't need to be asked twice. They filled plates with heaps of scrambled eggs and bread. Then they filled cups with fresh hot coffee and sat at a table.

A moment later, Tony came bounding down the stairs and went straight to the counter.

"Make mine over easy and can I get some milk for my coffee? That stuff Ivo ordered for me yesterday nearly gave me a coronary."

"I'm afraid we're all out of milk," said the Serb. The old man went to pick up some. There may be some creamer on the counter."

Suddenly, Tony realized it was the Serb behind the counter.

"You didn't strike me as the domestic type," said Tony.

"I am not. I am a lawyer. At least I was, before the war. I suppose that strictly speaking I still am but it's no longer how I make my living."

"If you don't mind my asking, how do you make your living?"

"You can ask," he answered.

"Nevermind," said Tony. "I mean you never even told me your name, why should you tell me what you do for a living?"

The Serb looked at him with an exasperated expression.

"My name is Petar; like the saint. Happy?"

"Ecstatic. You know, that reminds me of a story!"

"You know what, why don't we wait till the Croat wakes up and then you can tell your story to all of us? Besides, I think it would do us all a lot of good if we sit and have a little chat."

"Sounds good to me," said Tony.

That was good news, he thought. The Serb actually wanted to have a chat. *Maybe a good night's sleep got him thinking straight about this whole thing.* It only made sense. The Serb was sharp and resourceful. He must have realized that he stands to gain nothing by being everybody's enemy. *Now, if only Amir would relax his scruples just a hair.* He poured himself some coffee and looked around. Everyone was present except Ivo.

"By the way, anybody seen Marija? She up yet?" Tony asked. They all shook their heads. "Hmm... If it weren't for the old man, I'd go up and give her a little... incentive. If ya catch my drift?"

"Go ahead. The old man went into town for supplies," said Amir.

"He did?"

"Yes."

Tony thought he'd have a little fun with them. "Well then... perhaps I just might!"

"I don't think that is a good idea," said the Serb. "You'll only distract her."

"I agree, let her work, we don't have much time," said Itzak.

"Relax, guys! I'm just fucking with you!" said Tony. These guys have no sense of humor at all, he thought.

Just then, the front door opened and in walked Ivo and Marija! They were laughing and smiling and carrying bags of groceries. Tony's head almost exploded.

"Hey!" he said.

"Hey!" said Ivo. "*Dobar dan!*"

"*Dobar dan!*" said everybody except Tony. He rushed to Marija and grabbed her by the arms.

"What are you doing?" asked Tony.

"Ah, Tony! The sunshine was so bright and the birds were singing!"

"No, no, no! You need to get back to work. Unless...have you finished?"

"Not yet," she said. "But I will!"

"When?"

"Soon?"

His head was spinning. "OK, Marija, let me make this really clear. This is no game. We are leaving on a bus in just a little while, we need you to finish."

She nodded like a dejected schoolgirl. "I'm sorry. I'll get back to work."

"There's my girl! Now go! I'll come up and check on you in a little while."

She nodded and walked up the stairs. Tony turned to Ivo and found him lighting a cigarette.

"What's wrong with you?" he said.

"She's not your private property," said Ivo.

"I think you're missing Tony's point," said Itzak.

"I don't think so," he said, puffing on his cigarette. "I like her. She's nice. And besides, you're married, Tony. She deserved to know."

"Are you out of your fucking mind? Jesus Christ, you dumb fuck, don't you get it at all? She is completely irrelevant! The message is everything! And if she doesn't write it down before we leave, we're screwed!"

Ivo just continued to enjoy his smoke. "I'm in no rush."

"What? You miserable, ungrateful…"

That son of a bitch was trying to fuck him over. The thought caused something inside Tony to snap. He forgot himself and made a bull rush toward Ivo. But before he could take two steps, he was grabbed by Amir and Itzak, who had detected the meltdown coming before it hit critical.

"Fuck you! Fuck all of you! I knew I shouldn't trust you!" They held him by the arms trying to get him to calm down but it wasn't happening. "I should call the fucking U.S. Embassy! We'll see how you like that! You son of a bitch!"

"What the fuck are you yelling about?" said Ivo. "You're crazy!"

Just as the situation hit a boiling point, Petar began to laugh; first a chuckle, then a full belly laugh, then a demonic cackle almost falling over as he laughed. They looked at him in amazement. Somehow, in the supercharged atmosphere of anger and tension, he was laughing.

"You find this amusing?" said Itzak.

"More than you can imagine! And Tony, all I can say to you is: Welcome to the Balkans! I believe that for the first time since he arrived, our American friend has finally begun to understand what it's like to live here every day."

As he spoke, the Serb strolled over and placed a sheet of paper and a pen on each of the tables. Then he went back behind the counter.

"I don't like the way you were treating her. You need to learn respect," said Ivo.

"Shut up," said Tony.

"Yes," said Petar with a laugh. "Shut up!"

Ivo took the insult from the American, but he was not prepared to accept it from the Serb.

"And who's going to make me?" said Ivo.

Petar pulled the shotgun out from under the counter.

"Comrade Krupp, 12 gauge is going to make you."

They all looked at him in stunned silence.

"Put that down," said Itzak.

"With pleasure, as soon as you all sit down and put your hands face down on the table."

Tony wasn't paying attention, his focus was squarely on Ivo.

"Err...Tony?" said Petar.

Tony glanced at the Serb and noticed the shotgun. It was plot twist he hadn't anticipated.

"What the...holy shit!"

"Well said. The great orator seems to have lost his great gift of clever conversation. Now, do as I say, please. Amir, please sit here with Itzak."

They all sat down at the tables; Tony and Ivo at one and Amir and Itzak at the other.

"Good. In front of you is a contract. I have already signed both copies. Please sign it then hand it to the table next to you and sign again. Then, we will all have signed two copies."

"What does it say?" asked Amir.

"Does it matter, Turk? It is a Serb forcing you to do it so it must be evil, right?"

"What kind of contract is only two sentences long?" said Itzak.

"Just shut up and sign. I assure you it is legal and binding."

"I'm sure we can reasonably work this all out if you just..."

"But I thought you had it all reasoned out already? Last night? Remember?"

Silence filled the room. Tony's heart was racing. Suddenly, every story he'd ever heard or read about Serbian atrocities was running through his head.

"Only I am changing the terms somewhat," said Petar. "I am not looking to cut you all out. I am better than that. I have made us all equal partners. I'm not looking to make one cent more than any of you. But, I swear, I will not take one cent less either!"

"Look, there's no reason to do this," said Tony.

The Serb walked behind him and leaned over to speak directly into his ear: "If you do not shut up immediately, I will kill you. I have heard enough of your voice to last a lifetime. Now, sign!"

They all signed the contracts in front of them, then swapped sheets and signed again.

"Good. Now Itzak, please fold them in half and hand them to me." Itzak did as instructed and Petar placed them on the counter.

"Congratulations! We are now full limited liability partners. But...before we go on, I must say, I heard a lot of very unpleasant things said about me last night by my partners. Frankly, I longed to jump in and defend myself...but in the end I thought the prudent thing to do was to listen... and learn."

"To spy, to eavesdrop!" said Ivo.

"It's amusing to me, how you find the listening to bad things more offensive than the saying of them. You are a typical Croat in every way: loud, boring, stupid, violent."

"You should talk! A Serb! Ha!"

"Alright," said Petar. "I think it's time for the same rule that applies to Tony to apply to Ivo. One more word out of your mouth and I will shoot you."

"You're not going to kill someone simply for speaking?" said Itzak.

"Why not?" said Petar. "He killed people simply because they were at a soccer match!" He paused and let the statement sink in.

Tony's head was throbbing and he thought he might faint. He could feel his pulse in his ears, reverberating through his veins. This was no time to have a panic attack. He prayed that the longer the Serb talked, the greater the chance the old man would return. They had to keep him talking. But talking within this group usually led to arguments and arguments led to violence. Tony quickly decided he'd have to take the lead but he wasn't sure how.

His thoughts turned to Claire. He had hoped so desperately that she'd accompany him on this trip; thank God she hadn't. The shotgun pointed at the back of his head brought a lot of things into perspective. If he got out in one piece, he resolved to keep the promise he'd made to himself time and time again to work things out with Claire. Everything else was immaterial; he saw that now. But a rage-filled, Serbian with a shotgun stood in the way.

"In Krajina, where I am from," said Petar, "most Serbs deserted and went to Belgrade. The rich ones. Then they complained to the government that no one was protecting their homes for them! Do you know who wound up protecting the homes of the rich? Of course you do! The bastards too poor to leave! Like my family. Did any of you even know that half of the Yugoslav Army was actually *pressed* into service unwillingly?"

He walked behind the counter and folded the contracts up and put them in his pocket.

"My family stayed behind. Why, you ask? Because we never believed our Croat neighbors would ever do anything bad to us. But, just like Amir's school friend who turned on him, our friends and neighbors turned as well."

He came out from behind the counter and stood behind Ivo.

"What is wrong with Catholics, anyway? Have all your child-molesting priests fucked up your heads so badly that you have no values anymore?"

"Ha! Serbs are fine teachers of values!" said Ivo.

"Since I have the gun, today, I am the teacher. And the lesson for today is "Why all Catholics are Homosexuals and Child-molesters.""

He tapped the barrel of the gun against Ivo's head. "I'm sorry, did you say something? Come on, say it!"

Ivo just shook his head.

"Don't you know anything? All the child molesting priests are in the United States, you moron!"

The Serb viciously cracked Ivo in the back of the head with the butt of the shotgun making an awful sound.

Amir looked at Itzak and whispered, "Yeah, so much for crosses taking care of crosses."

"An interesting proposition," said Petar. "All the child molesting priests are in the United States. Hmm."

"Now, wait a minute," said Tony.

"No one told you to speak," said Petar, waving the gun in Tony's direction. "I think the Croat makes a very good point."

"Oh, please! Lemme guess, another country with no homosexuals, right? I'll tell you something you all have in common: denial!"

"Oh, please," said Ivo, "America has way more faggots than Croatia."

"Well, *gee* Ivo," said Tony sarcastically, "in all fairness, it is a much larger country."

"All right. Shut up! I'm tired of both of you!" said Petar.

Suddenly, something snapped in Tony's mind.

"Fuck you! Shoot me!" said Tony. "You're probably gonna kill us all anyway, but I'm sick of this bullshit! You hate me 'cuz I'm American; tough shit, get over it. You think all Catholics are child molesters? Pedophiles are pedophiles, you fucking moron! It's a disease, not a religion! You hate Bill Clinton and America because we waited so long to intervene here, well, guess what? At least we came! When the rest of the fucking world turned its back on you, at least we came! It may have been too little, too late, I don't know, but at least we came. We didn't stand to gain shit from helping you except the knowledge that we did the right thing. You guys love your little expressions, well I got an old American expression for all of you: It's never too late to do the right thing!"

Petar cracked Tony in the back of the head with the butt of the shotgun. The blow nearly knocked him unconscious, but the pain prevented it. He had trouble focusing his eyes and he thought he might throw up. He turned his thoughts to Claire and to the kids at the home in Tuzla and it helped him focus.

"Well what do you know?" said Petar. "The American has grown a pair! But you know what? You all deserve each other. Backstabbing, two-timing. You sick twisted... agh! You want to know why I hate Croats? Croats shot and killed my three year old nephew in Krajina and left his body in the street! In the street! You all talk about how horrible the war was for you, well let me tell you, for Serbs it was no picnic either! I'm sick and tired of hearing horror stories! After a while they all begin to sound the same."

Tony was dazed from the blow but he needed to keep him talking. He wanted to diffuse the anger level if possible, because he saw the Serb starting to boil over and that would mean bad news for all of them. Before he could say another word, Itzak chimed in.

"I think the world has never heard the Serbian side of…"

"Shut up! I'm sick of you, too! You are very smart but you think you know it all," said Petar. "Your words are full of deceit! Oh, they sound nice and they fall smoothly from your tongue, but they are lies! You and your little Muslim friend are very fond of quoting scripture as if somehow it makes you better than the rest of us. Well, it's not how much scripture you can quote that counts! It's how much you live your life according to it! There's more to salvation than a little bit of foreskin!"

"Said the man holding the shotgun," said Tony.

Petar wrapped him on the back of the head with the butt of the gun again and Tony winced in pain. This time Tony just about blacked out and sat lifeless in his chair. The Serb continued.

"You asked if it mattered to me if you were a Jew? Well, it did. And it does. There were over a thousand Jews living in Belgrade before the NATO bombings in 1999. But somehow, for some reason, they all decided to leave the city just before the air strikes occurred. How did they know when the strikes would happen? And why didn't they tell anyone? Last night you spoke of the 'death of trust,' remember? You discussed it right before you agreed to fuck me over! You Goddamn hypocrite! Do you know how to say 'fuck you' in Hebrew? Two simple words: Trust me!"

He wound up as if to hit Itzak with the butt end of the gun but stopped.

"But then I learned that you were not really Slovenian at all! You are actually an American!"

They all looked at Itzak in confusion. He just stared straight ahead.

"That's right, my friends! He is American! Another poor disillusioned American coming here to tell us how quaint our ways are and to take all he can steal from us. The Jews may have managed to convert the U.S. into one great big Zionist tool, herding stupid Americans around like cattle; starting wars against one people after another, while Israel quietly sells weapons to their enemies!" He stood right behind Itzak and spoke directly to him. "Luckily, here we have no such problem. We eliminated our Jewish problems years ago." He then stood up with renewed swagger. "And best yet, he's a fucking thief! On the run from the law! That's correct, my friends, for all his bullshit intellectualism, he is nothing more than a common thief on the run!"

"Is that true?" asked Tony.

"It's complicated," said Itzak.

Ivo burst out laughing. "I kind of like you more now!"

"Mr. High and Mighty, who couldn't resist judging everyone else is a common criminal," said the Serb.

"My friend," said Itzak slowly and deliberately. "I am truly sorry for you. For your heart is black and you are blind with hate."

"And if my heart is black, who blackened it? How did it get that way? Watching the Muslim and the Jew "bonding" last night was very very touching, in fact, I might have shed a tear if it were not for the fact that what bonded them was treachery! Greed! Conspiracy to lie, to steal, to cheat!"

His speech was so curt and so bombastic that the silence that followed seems to almost have an echo to it. Itzak spoke softly.

"If that is all you heard last night, then..."

"No, my friend, I heard plenty more. But you said it best! We are a diseased species. We are not moving closer to perfection, we're going in the opposite direction."

"Perhaps," said Itzak.

"No! Not perhaps! We don't live in the 'perhaps' and in the 'maybe.' We live in the present, in the here and now. Why bother pretending we are something we are not? Pretend we are friends? Pretend we can ever be friends? Pretend we can ever work together."

Exhausted from his rant, he dropped into a chair next to the bar. He struggled to pull a cigarette out of its package and light it, while still holding the gun on them. He took a long deep drag and blew a vast cleansing cloud of smoke into the air. If his face betrayed anything, it was now profound sadness rather than rage.

In spite of all, Tony couldn't help feeling sorry for the guy. He remembered an incident that happened on his earlier trip. He was hesitant to bring it up. He wasn't sure if it was appropriate or not, or even if it might cause Petar to blow, but he determined he had to roll the dice and tell his story, in hope that it might have the same kind of profound effect on them that it had had on him.

"Petar, my friend," Tony said in a tiny voice. "You are wrong. And I know you are because I've seen it with my own eyes. On my first trip here I visited Split. I was in one of those bars along the promenade in the port when it happened. There was a big screen TV showing a concert of some kind of folk music. A group of ten guys wearing traditional costumes with red sashes around their waists and singing harmony *a capella*."

"That's called klapa music, it's been around for over a thousand years," said Ivo. "It's the songs of the Dalmatian sailors."

"It was very powerful hearing the mens' voices all blending

together in those complex harmonies, even though I didn't understand a word they were singing. But as powerful as it was, it was nothing compared to what happened in the bar. There were about a dozen guys in the bar who suddenly went completely silent when the song began. One of the guys was our Serbian travel agent, one was the Bosnian driver we'd hired, there were at least a pair of Albanian Kosovars and the rest I assume were locals, Croats. But as the band sang, I sensed something strange and wonderful was happening and looked around the bar to see pair after pair of eyes wet with the tears they were fighting back. I whispered to my guide: 'what's going on?' He whispered back: 'this is an old Yugoslav folk song. It has profound meaning to all of us.' I asked: 'what are they saying?' And he said: 'the chorus of the song says: "Why God, will we suffer death before we are willing to say 'I'm sorry?' Oprosti.'"

Tony noticed audible gasps from all of them.

"Then at the end of the song, the singers all began to chant the same line over and over, louder and louder, and suddenly all of the men in the bar stood up, and sang along. When it was over, they sat back down. The hair on the back of my neck was standing.

"I asked what was that they were singing? And the guide said the final line in the song is: "Stand up, turn to the man next to you, and tell him: *I'm sorry*.'"

Silence hung around them for several minutes.

"Is peace really so unbearable?" said Itzak wistfully.

"Shut up. My head hurts," said the Serb. "I need a cigarette."

He looked for one in his pack but it was empty. He crumpled it up and threw it on the floor. Then he went behind the counter and took a pack. He opened it and lit one. Then he walked out, staggering as he went and stood behind them. Tony was more nervous than before. The story clearly touched a nerve with every one of them, but now the Serb looked like he was done, and Tony was afraid he might just end the game.

"Why…why launch a war with so much vigor and so much propaganda and then abandon your boys?" said Petar, almost crying, the shotgun shaking in his hands. "So much blood, so much…so much." He walked over to the counter and leaned against it. "You all wanted to know if I am an atheist? You wanted to know if I am a believer or an infidel? So you could fuck me over with a clear conscience? Well, I was a good Christian once. Kept holy the Sabbath. Fasted during Lent. Received all the sacraments. So, why do I come to Medjugorje? Why?"

He paused and leaned over toward Tony and crazily started humming the *Jeopardy!* theme.

"Why? To visit my brother, who lies buried there. No visions, no Virgins, no messages, no ulterior motives. Just to spend some time with him and to keep his grave clean."

"The same grass that grows on his grave also grows in the cemetery in Srebrenica," said Itzak.

"You all said the story of the Serbian soldier roasted alive was propaganda…I can tell you…it was not. It is true. I was a good Christian once… but no more…all my faith is gone."

Amir slapped his hands on the table and turned to Tony.

"Well? Have you heard enough? Do you believe me now?"

"Huh?" said Tony.

"Now do you believe he's an atheist? He just said so."

"Shut up, both of you!" cried the Serb.

"I guess," whispered Tony.

Amir stood up and turned around.

"Good. I was about to puke listening to this bullshit."

"Don't move, Turk!"

Amir slowly walked toward Petar.

"No. I don't care if you shoot me."

"Amir sit down!" said Tony.

"I will if you don't sit down," said Petar.

"I bet you will. I bet nothing would make you happier than for me to give you an excuse to blow my head off."

"Don't think I won't!"

"Amir! Sit the fuck down!" cried Tony.

"Please, Amir!" begged Itzak.

"What do all you Serbs say?" asked Amir. "Better to die in battle than live in shame?" He kept moving closer and Petar kept backing up.

"Don't be stupid, Amir! He's not worth it!" said Ivo.

"One more step, Turk and I swear it will be your last," said Petar, lifting the gun up to his shoulder.

"If we rush him, he can't shoot all of us!" said Ivo.

"But, he doesn't want to shoot all of us. Just me. Isn't that right, Chetnik?"

"One more step and so help me…"

"—*God?* Isn't that how it goes? So help me God? But you don't believe in God. You don't believe in anything! So, go ahead, pull the trigger! Do it! Do it!" Amir screamed.

He lunged toward Petar, who backed up against the counter and fired. But nothing happened. He pulled the trigger again, and again nothing happened. It only clicked and clicked.

"What the...?" said Tony.

"Relax, boys," said Amir. "You don't really think I'm stupid enough to leave a loaded shotgun around with a Serb in the house do you?" Saying that, he pulled the shells out of his pocket and threw them on the floor.

At that instant, Ivo leapt up and tackled Petar and wrestled the gun away from him. Then, he hit him across the face with the butt end, knocking him to the floor. As Petar tried to crawl away, Ivo kept kicking and kicking him until Tony grabbed him and pulled him away.

"You fucking cocksucker! You animal!" said Ivo. "You don't deserve the message from God! You don't deserve the blessing of our Lady!" He tried to break free from Tony's grip but Itzak stood before him blocking his way.

Finally, Petar, bruised and bloodied, reached the door and managed to stand up. He was dazed and bleeding from the mouth. He wiped his mouth with a handkerchief and tried to compose himself.

"You're all hypocrites!" he said, seething. "Liars! Backstabbers! None of you will ever see a single mark from your Virgin. None of you! I curse you all! I curse you!" He staggered out the door into the parking lot.

"He doesn't believe in God yet he believes in curses," said Amir.

"Pft! What a hypocrite!" said Ivo, as he grabbed the Serb's coat from the chair. He walked over to the door, opened it and threw it out at him. Tony wanted to rush after Petar to make sure he was ok, but then he thought better of it. He sat down and tried to stop his hands from shaking but he couldn't.

Amir spied the two contracts on the floor. They must have fallen out of Petar's pocket. He picked them up then pulled out his lighter and burned them.

Yelling could be heard outside. Ivo went to the door to see what it was. The old man was outside with the bags of supplies and he was arguing with Petar.

"The old guy is worried Petar is skipping out on his tab."

Suddenly, the old man came through the front door in a fury. Like a freight train, he blew right past them without a word and went straight into the kitchen. A moment later he burst from the kitchen with a giant meat cleaver in his hands.

"Give me the gun! Now!" he yelled. Ivo handed it to him gently.

"Relax! Relax!" said Itzak.

"Now, get out!" he cried.

"Look. It's okay! It's okay!" said Tony.

He held the meat cleaver menacingly high and poised to strike.

"I said, get out! Now!"

"You don't understand!" implored Itzak. "Please, listen!"

But he was past the point of listening.

At that moment, Marija ran down the stairs and pleaded with her father in Bosnian. The argument was beyond heated, but the girl would not back down. Finally, he reluctantly nodded in agreement.

"Papa says you can stay. But only until bus comes! Then you go!"

They all nodded and thanked the old man.

PETER DANISH

"When is the bus due?" asked Ivo.

"About an hour," said Marija.

"Yikes!" said Tony. "Go! Finish! Hurry!"

She obediently rushed up the stairs and back to work.

"Do you think she'll make it?" asked Amir.

"She better," said Tony with a nervous laugh, "because that old guy means business!"

CHAPTER 17

THE MIRACLE

Friday, 10:00am

The moment Marija left, they sat back down around the tables.

"Okay, we've got a shitload we need to discuss and very little time," said Tony. "So, at the risk of being callous, first let's talk about how we spread the news? Or should we test it first?"

"I think we're putting the cart before the horse," said Itzak.

"And another very important point," Tony carried on, "are we all going to stay in Bosnia to do this? Because I need to plan."

"Wait a minute," said Amir, "are we planning to just steal it from Marija?"

"No, of course not," said Ivo. "We must make her an equal partner."

"This girl has known this secret for years now without seeking to make a cent from it. Why do you think suddenly she will be interested in money?" asked Itzak.

"Respectfully, Itzak," said Tony, "I doubt very much she ever even considered the magnitude of this discovery and its potential windfall."

"Here we go again!" said Amir. "I have no problem getting rich, believe me. But this is not some commodity! This is a gift from God!"

"Unfortunately, Amir is right," said Itzak. "This is not a decision to be taken lightly or made in haste." Tony rolled his eye and tapped his foot impatiently. "And frankly, Tony, you can behave like a petulant child all you like, it won't change my mind."

"Guys, I totally agree!" said Tony. "Another time and another place and we would do it differently. But there's no time!"

"We need to have a discussion with Marija and possibly with her father as well," said Amir.

"Oh, geez, that's great!" said Tony.

"Look Tony, the world will keep spinning with or without us learning this secret," said Amir.

"Guys, haven't you heard the old axiom about 'being ready when opportunity knocks?' Well, it's knocking!" said Tony. "But it won't be for long! This might be the only chance any of us ever have to make a meaningful change in our lives! In the lives of our families! Just think all the good you could do for the ones you love! Do it for them! For God's sake, let's not blow it and spend the rest of our lives regretting it!"

A hush fell over them. The ideological impasse threatened to ruin everything. It would take a miracle to get them all to agree.

Just then, a noise was heard outside.

"What's that?" said Tony.

Ivo rushed to the window. "It's the bus!" he said.

"Shit! He's early!" cried Tony. "No way Marija's even close to done yet. We gotta stall somehow! Let's think."

At that moment, the door flew open and the bus driver came in followed by his assistant, but he looked completely different. He was glowing with elation. The gruff old driver was positively beaming!

"*Dobar dan*, brothers! And Hallelujah!" He shook his fists in front of them all and looked like he was about to cry.

"You missed it! You all missed it!" he said.

"What? What did we miss?" said Tony.

"Everything! You have no idea!"

The old man entered with his cleaver in his hand.

"OK, bus is here! Pack you bags and get out!"

"Wait a second! Listen to what the driver is telling us," said Tony.

The old man turned to the driver in confusion.

"I wouldn't have believed it if I hadn't seen it with my own eyes!" said the driver.

"Tell us!" said Ivo.

"It was the most extraordinary vision in years! Praise God!" said the driver and he and the assistant blessed themselves. Itzak gently pulled the old man to the table to listen with them.

"As I said, if I had not witnessed it with my own eyes I never would have believed it. The entire canton is talking. Have you not heard?"

"*Sto*? What happened?" said the old man.

"Mirjana herself attended and saw a vision! An incredible vision!"

"She is a saint!" said the old man sitting on a chair next to the driver. Tony saw this and ran over to the stairs to check on Marija's progress.

"The mayor of Medjugorje was present and he declared the day in Mirjana's name and gave her a formal proclamation."

"Ah, the mayor!" said Amir sarcastically.

"But the vision! The vision!" said Ivo.

"I still can't believe the mayor was there," said Amir, rolling his eyes.

"My heart can barely take it. Ten years I've been driving this route and never, never has anything like this ever happened!"

"What? What happened?" cried the old man.

The driver took a deep breath and let it out. Then he spoke, "Now listen closely…"

"Done!" yelled Marija from the stairs and all eyes turned to her. "It's finished!"

Everyone except the old man turned away from the bus driver in unison. Marija ran to Tony and gave him the paper.

"This is it?" he asked, breathlessly.

"Yes! I rushed it just for you!"

"Ah Marija, that's wonderful! Now step back," he said as he, Amir, Ivo, and Itzak furiously tried to read the contents.

"Remember," she said, "it is all in metaphors so read carefully."

"I don't care if it's in braille!" said Tony as he began to read. He sat next to Itzak and Ivo and Amir looked on over his shoulders. In only a few seconds, they were all squinting and scratching their heads in confusion.

"So you were saying?" said the old man.

"There was a miracle," said the bus driver solemnly. "A miracle!"

Itzak jerked his head toward the bus driver.

"What did you say?" he asked, with excitement.

"I said a miracle," he said again.

"Yeah, yeah, that's great," said Tony absently. "What does this say here? I can hardly read her writing."

"What do you mean?" asked Amir.

"Mirjana performed not one, but two miracles! Two! Two miracles! And Mirjana is the reason. Mirjana! She should be sainted!"

"Please, what happened?" implored Itzak.

"There was a young boy, not more than ten years old, he had a club foot," said the driver. "They say he had been a cripple his entire life. When Mirjana saw him in the crowd, she was so moved she called him forward and blessed him. And he tossed away his crutch and could walk freely again!"

The old man and the driver's assistant blessed themselves.

"Did you hear that, Tony?" said Amir.

"Yeah, yeah club foot. What word is this?"

"It looks like some kind of a recipe," said Ivo.

"What was the second miracle?" asked the old man.

"Oh my God! Maybe it's a cleanse! The 'Holy Virgin Cleanse!' I love it!" said Tony.

"I'm confused," said Amir. "It says in the introduction here that Ivanka got the message, didn't you say it was Mirjana?"

"Hmm?" said Marija, "Ah, I can't remember. It was a long time… wait, yes, it was definitely Mirjana!"

"So, as I was saying," continued the driver, "Mirjana needed to rest after the first healing and needed a drink, after all, she's not as young as she used to be."

"Ya, of course," said the old man, "Understandable. How old is she now, I forget?"

"Hmm...I guess she must be around forty by now," said the driver.

"Uh huh," said the old man. "That sounds about right."

Approximately two seconds later, Itzak froze. He slowly lifted his gaze up from Marija's letter and with a look of terror in his eyes, a terror that ran down to his heart, mechanically, he turned to the driver.

"I'm sorry," he said, "*how old did you say she was?*"

"Around forty, I think," said the driver.

Slowly, Itzak turned and looked at Marija. She was chewing gum and fixing her hair in the mirror, looking very much like the teenager she was.

"Wait a minute!" said Amir. "Marija just said, that it was Mirjana..."

"Mirjana, Ivanka, what does it matter?" snapped Tony.

"So," said the driver, clearing his throat, "as I was saying..."

"Forgive me, one last time, sir," said Itzak to the old man, "But, how old is your daughter?"

"Marija? She is seventeen. Why?"

Itzak began to feel pain in his chest. His breathing grew labored.

"And how old was she when you moved here from Medjugorje?"

"Medjugorje?" said the old man. "We never lived in Medjugorje. We live in this house our whole life. I built it myself."

CHAPTER 18

REVELATIONS

Friday, 10:30am

Itzak stared at the old man, then at Marija, then at the old man again. The other men keep working on the letter. Itzak was now perspiring profusely and on the verge of tears.

"Are you absolutely *sure* you've never lived in Medjugorje?" he pleaded.

"Of course I am sure! Never."

Itzak closed his eyes as he sank down in his chair, and his entire world was one notch closer to midnight. He groaned a loud primal groan as he wiped his hands down his face.

"Wanna keep it down? We're trying to decipher this mess."

Amir looked up for a moment and glanced over at Itzak, whose face was ashen.

"What's the matter?" said Amir.

"What's the matter?" said Itzak, with a chuckle. "What's the matter? I am a dead man."

"So, once again," said the driver, louder and more annoyed than before, "as I was saying!"

"Okay, look, pal, I hate to be rude," said Tony, "but could you put a sock in it for just minute? We really need to concentrate here and we don't have much time."

The driver stared at Tony, deeply insulted. He got up and walked to the door.

"Fine. Five minutes and we leave," he said, and he went outside. His assistant followed close behind.

"This makes no sense at all!" said Ivo. "It must be written in some kind of dialect."

"Itzak, you're the damn scholar, would you please give us a hand? We're dying here!" said Tony.

"Ah, the irony," said Itzak as he slowly got up from his chair and stood behind Tony. He looked at them, furiously trying to decipher the message and chuckled to himself. *By the time they figure it out I'll be playing a harp.*

He leaned over Tony's shoulder and read. After a moment, something appeared to come over him. He looked gravely at the letter and his jaw dropped. His eyes bulged out of his head and his hand covered his mouth in shock.

"What? What is it?" said Tony

Itzak grabbed the letter from him and started feverishly reading it to himself.

"Of course!" he said.

"Of course, what?" said Tony.

"My God! I see it!

"You do?" cried Ivo.

"Yes! How did I miss this before!"

"What? Say it!"

"It's all perfectly clear to me now!" said Itzak lost in a sense of wonder.

"Tell us! Damn it!" cried Tony.

Itzak stood before them beaming, almost crying, then he very dramatically read the letter aloud.

"It says, 'Dear Friends, on Easter Sunday, our Lord Jesus Christ rolled away the stone and came forth from the tomb."

He paused and looked around at their transfixed faces.

"And…if he should see his shadow, we will have six more weeks of winter.'"

It took a second for his words to sink in.

"What?" said Tony.

"But! It says here, that if he should see the Easter Bunny, we will have an early frost. And then, he must then notify Santa Claus and give him a storm warning. This is the word of God. Amen."

"What the fuck are you talking about?" said Tony.

"This! This! It is bullshit! It's a fake!" cried Itzak, manically. "She doesn't know the children! She never knew the children. She never lived in Medjugorje! She didn't go to school with them! For Christ's sake, she's twenty years younger than they are!"

If the room had been completely empty it could not have been more silent. They sat for a minute, mouths agape as reality set in.

"Holy shit," said Tony.

"Precisely," said Itzak, laughing maniacally. "Holy shit, indeed! Truer words were never spoken!"

Tony looked at Marija, who strolled over with a big grin on her face. His heart was pumping so loud he could hear it in his ears. He could barely breathe. She just smiled.

"Marija?" he said feebly.

"Eh? Eh? You see?" she said with a flirtatious wink. "I am *good* actress!"

"Wha-?"

"I fool you completely! Yes?"

"But…"

"Now you know I can act, you put me in your movie? Take me to America?"

Tony was hyperventilating. His entire world was unraveling.

"But…"

"Yes?"

"But…but…the Crucifix?"

"Ach… I get it at Holy Virgin gift shop."

"But…but…the formula?"

"Old Bosnian beef stew recipe."

"But…but…but…ah, shit!" he said and collapsed onto the table. His heart felt as though an icy hand was grabbing it. He nearly wept.

CHAPTER 19

LOOSE ENDS

Friday, 11:00am

The sound of the bus horn was blaring out in the parking lot.

"Okay! Two minutes!" yelled the driver from outside.

The old man stood up and loudly cleared his throat.

"You better get your things, or he will leave without you," he said.

But they were all still too much in shock to even react. The old man grabbed his daughter's arm and dragged her over to the stairs and pointed up at them with the cleaver. She looked at Tony, pouted for a minute, then ran upstairs.

As they sat there in suspended animation, the old man walked over to the table. He whistled and tapped the table with his cleaver. Once he had their attention, he smiled and pointed to the door.

For a minute, Tony bore his suffering silently. Then, in a wistfully shell-shocked voice he broke the silence.

"I don't believe it," he said, lost in his own world, his passion worn out.

"I guess we better get our bags," said Ivo nodding at the old man.

"It was all a fake," said Tony.

"I'll give you a hand," said Amir in a purely business-like manner, as he and Ivo left and went upstairs.

Tony's mind raced. *It couldn't be all bullshit! It just couldn't be!*

"It can't be! It can't!" said Tony. "I mean, it just can't. I trusted her. I trusted her completely."

"And on that delicate impulse you proceeded. Trust makes us vulnerable, Tony," said Itzak, wistfully. "And greed makes us gullible. In the end, we believe to be true, what we want to be true."

Tony snapped back from his other world and looked at Itzak like he was insane.

"Well, *gee* Itzak, you're being awfully philosophically about it."

"What choice do I have?" said Itzak, fighting back a yawn. "You seem to think that your faith has somehow entitled you to something. What you still need to learn, and no one can show you, is that faith is its own reward."

He reached over and squeezed Tony's hand.

"It's really very simple: every morning when we wake up, we really only have one decision to make: am I going to make the world a little bit brighter today, or am I going to make the world a little bit darker today? That's it. I learned that when I got my cancer diagnosis. And for me, it was facing death that gave me the courage to face life once again."

Tony swallowed hard and scratched his head.

"Yeah. I guess you're right. Actually, I know you're right! It's just a little bit hard to think that way right now." Tony exhaled toward the ceiling and held his face in his hands. "But you believed her too, didn't you?"

"I certainly wanted to! You were not a fool, Tony, relax. The madness infected us all. As far as believing goes, I think that there exists a very fine line between faith and belief, and each of us must decide where we draw that line for ourselves."

Tony looked around. He simply couldn't believe just how cavalier they all seemed to be in the face of this mammoth revelation. They just took it in stride. They had had fame, fortune, everything they could ever have wanted dangled in front of them and then callously snatched away in one big joke!

"Seriously, I don't get it. Am I the only one totally freaked out by this? Where's the shock? Where's the anger? Where's the outrage? Doesn't anybody even care?"

Itzak stood up and gently patted Tony on the shoulders.

"These people are used to disappointment. One more is no big deal. They kind of expect it. In fact, they are usually shocked when things actually turn out for the best!"

The thought made sense and Tony slowly began to understand. After all, he wasn't really all he'd led them to believe, was he? It was sort of a vain misrepresentation to suggest he was famous or successful. They had fallen for his window dressing… and now he had fallen for hers. It was folly to pretend he was not disappointed but perhaps he could learn something from the impassive stoicism of his fellow pilgrims.

"How long has it been since you called your wife?" asked Itzak.

"What? Forever," Tony grunted. "I wouldn't even know what to say."

Itzak placed a hand on Tony's shoulder.

"Often, the most important part of communication isn't what

you say, but the mere fact that you made contact, that you reached out. I strongly suspect that if your wife is half the woman you've said she is, she would find the events of the last twenty four hours enchanting if not positively hilarious!"

Tony smiled. *The last twenty four hours! Imagine that!* He had gone through the entire gamut of human emotions in the last twenty four hours. But Itzak was dead right, Claire would friggin' love this story. And maybe, he just might have a great screenplay in his hands after all!

"You ought to be a producer!" said Tony. "You have great instincts. Think of it: *Gorgeous, mysterious, young girl completely dupes greedy old men*—it's practically already written!"

"Not just yet. The final act has yet to be written," said Itzak.

He stood up and called out to the old man in Croatian. The old man came over and they had a brief but extremely animated discussion. The old man pointed at Tony and violently shook his head "*no!*" Even Tony could see that. But Itzak smiled and patted the old man on the shoulder. He then took out some bills from his wallet and handed them to him. The old man took the money, but he still didn't look happy. They spoke for another minute; this time Itzak appeared to be reprimanding the old man. Finally, they shook hands and laughed. The old man turned and went up the stairs, counting the money as he walked.

Itzak picked up the deck of cards from the counter and sat back down with Tony.

"What the hell was that about?" asked Tony.

"I asked him when the next bus to Medjugorje was due."

"And?"

Itzak took the cards out of the case and shuffled them.

"Same time tomorrow," he said. "I booked us on it."

"You what? Us?"

"Yes. The four of us."

"Four?"

"You know, Tony, our own personal bitterness and sense of futility really does nothing to change the basic possibility that reignites for all us every day. Some days it's impossible to see, and we may not believe it, but it's there just the same, waiting for someone else to grasp at."

Tony marveled at the pearls of wisdom bestowed upon him, but rolled his eyes just the same.

"Okay, but you didn't answer my question. The four of us?"

"Well, Ivo desperately needs to make his confession. And I've got to make certain that Amir doesn't do anything stupid and ruin his entire life."

"And me?"

"You, Tony, you need to have a little more magic in your life. I do, too."

Tony looked at him incredulously for a moment, then smiled.

"You know what, Itzak? I'll bet you were a really wonderful rabbi. No... you *are* a wonderful rabbi."

Amir and Ivo came rushing down the stairs followed by the old man.

"You booked us for another night?" asked Amir.

"Do you know how to play brishcula?" asked Itzak, ignoring his question.

"Of course," said Ivo. Amir nodded as well.

"Then sit. I've already dealt you in."

They shrugged their shoulders and sat, too tired to argue. Tony adjusted his cards.

"Brishcula?" he said, blinking his eyes. "You do realize I'm completely clueless here, right?"

"I realized that the moment I met you," said Itzak with a wink.

"You think there's any chance of another miracle in Medjugorje tomorrow?" asked Amir.

"After two miracles today? Pft, doubtful," said Ivo.

"Well, one can always hope," said Itzak.

Itzak continued to deal the cards and they began to play, though it was clear that their minds were anywhere but on the game.

"Hey, so what was the second miracle anyway?" asked Amir.

"The driver never said," said Tony.

"Hmm. It really does make you think," said Amir.

"It sure does," said Ivo. "About what? Oh, wait. I get it. It's creepy!"

"Creepy?"

"Yeah, in the end, the Serb's curse came true. Creepy. How do you think he knew?"

"I think he was a little better at math than we were," said Itzak.

Although on one level he wanted to cry, the storyteller inside him couldn't help but see the humor in their situation, and instinctively Tony knew he must write it all down.

"She wants to be an actress," Tony laughed.

"It's almost like Chaucer," said Itzak. "*The Wife of Bath's Tale,* I believe."

Suddenly there was a gasp at the stairs. They turned and it was Marija.

"Tony! Ivo!' she called out, elated to see them. She rushed toward them but her father cut her off and grabbed her. He angrily pointed back to the stairs and after a petulant minute, Marija reluctantly went back, pouting all the way. She stopped on the first step of the stairs and turned to them.

"You won't forget me when you get back to Hollywood, will you Tony?" she asked.

Tony put down his cards and turned in his seat. He looked at her and smiled.

"Oh, no. I won't forget you! You can count on it! Not one word, not one gesture of yours shall I, could I, ever forget!"

Marija ran up the stairs like a school girl in love.

Amir and Itzak just exchanged confused glances.

"That's from *Anna Karenina,* in case you're wondering," said Tony with a wink as he turned back and reexamined his cards.

Itzak looked at Tony with incredulous amazement.

"You read *Anna Karenina*?" he asked.

Tony laughed. "As if... I saw the movie."

"Of course you did," said Itzak, shaking his head and trying unsuccessfully not to smile.

They resumed the game and in the distance, they heard the bus beep its horn once more.

"*Dovidjenja,*" said Ivo, sadly.

"I think it's better to live not knowing things, not having all the answers," said Amir. "I don't feel the need to know all the answers, and I'm not frightened by not knowing them. Mystery is one of the greatest things in life."

"Maybe," said Itzak, looking at his cards. "Some things need to be reserved for future generations to discover, to insure they have their share of mysteries. God, Allah, Mother Nature, whatever the name, she doesn't choose to reveal all her cards at once."

"The world is capricious, Tony," said Amir. "It does us no good to rail against it. We must simply accept it with as much fortitude as we can find."

Tony glanced around the table and rolled his eyes at all the highfalutin wisdom they were spouting. Maybe that's what got them through all the tough times. It might not be a bad idea to try a bit more of it himself. He also realized that he'd begun to feel a genuine affection for the three of them. He hoped they'd all stay in touch at the conclusion of their little adventure, but he doubted it. He even felt a pang of regret for Petar. *He was a jackass, and a little bit crazy, but in the end, they did screw him over.* Tony thought of the miserable life the poor guy must have had and felt especially bad when he realized that had he not practically forced the Serb to join in the discussion, the guy would probably be peacefully on his way to Medjugorje right now. It was yet another reminder of how unpredictable and ultimately unfair life was.

"Your eyes have that faraway look," said Itzak. "What is it?"

Tony debated with himself for a moment. He wasn't sure he wanted to go there, but he couldn't keep silent.

"I was thinking about Petar."

"Why?" asked Ivo, rolling his eyes.

"Because he feels guilty about the way we treated him. That's right, isn't it?" said Amir.

"Sorta, but mostly I was thinking if I hadn't baited him and tricked him into playing our game, he'd... well, he'd probably be a whole lot better off right now."

"You did him a favor. And *Brisc!*" called out Ivo, slamming down his cards with a hearty laugh. "I win," he said as he gathered and started to shuffle the cards again.

"How do you figure that?" asked Tony.

"You saved him the complete *humiliation* of being duped and made to look like a fool by a young girl."

"That's a very good point. I guess. I still feel bad."

Itzak reached out and touched Tony's hand.

"Tony, my friend. In this case, guilt is good. Not because you are really guilty of anything, but because feeling bad now will make you feel good in the long run."

Tony scratched his head. These guys, he thought, had a profound understanding of life that he could never touch. But were they better off for it?

"When we feel guilty about something, we proceed under the foolish misconception that we are solely responsible for something," said Itzak. "And if we feel that we are responsible, then we feel that we could have prevented it. That idea is pleasing to us because it suggests that we really have some control over our lives; that we are not just passively observing the events of our lives blowing past us like a movie. You think you treated the Serb unfairly, maybe you did. Maybe we all did. But he was not particularly pleasant either, remember. How's that bump on your head?"

"Don't remind me!"

"The point is, we all fall down. Some think that getting back up is what really matters, but I think helping up the fellow who has fallen is the harder, and braver choice."

Amir looked at Itzak with tear-filled eyes. Itzak blushed.

"Forgive me, I'm starting to talk like a rabbi again."

"No, Itzak," said Tony. "It's like you said. Once you are a rabbi, you are always a rabbi. I think you really need to be with your congregation again."

Itzak smiled. "In time. In time."

They played in silence for a moment or two when Ivo started to laugh.

"What's so funny?" said Tony.

"Us. An hour ago, we all thought we were going to be rich!"

They all started to laugh.

"It's amazing how your entire world can change in the space of an hour," said Amir.

"You know," said Ivo, "there's an old Croatian expression that goes: 'Until this moment, I never understood how hard it was to lose something I never had.'"

Tony had to think about that one for a minute.

"Actually, sorry to say, I think that's a Bosnian expression," said Amir.

"I think it's a Yiddish expression," said Itzak.

"I think he just made it up!" said Tony. "Let me tell you, I learned a lot about you people in the last twenty-four hours! First rule: never play poker with a Bosnian woman! Second, no matter your geographical differences, no matter your ethnic differences, no matter your religious differences—deep down you're all pretty much the same—you're all a bunch of capitalists!"

"Amen," said Itzak.

As they continued to play cards silently, the old man turned on the radio behind the bar. Ivo whistled to Tony and jerked his head toward the radio.

"Recognize it?" he said. It was *"Oprosti"* by Gibonni. The old man wiped down the counter with a towel and hummed along.

Itzak motioned to him to bring over some wine. The old man nodded and took out four glasses and a jug of red wine. He poured the wine and place the glasses on their table.

Itzak raised a glass and made a toast.

"Here's to miracles!" he toasted. They all clinked glasses.

"To miracles!" they toasted and sipped their wine.

The driver's assistant quietly returned from outside in the parking lot. He walked over to the counter and leaned against it.

He whistled, as he always did, to get the old man's attention. Then he pointed to the cigarettes. The old man handed him a pack and the assistant paid him. As he turned around and leaned against the bar, the assistant pulled out and lit a cigarette. Nobody even seemed to be aware of his presence. He took a long deep, satisfied drag on the cigarette, then he cleared his throat and let out a deep smokers' cough as he walked to the door.

"You forgot your change!" said the old man.

The assistant stopped, turned halfway and smiled.

"Keep it!" he said with a wink, in a perfectly normal voice, without his vocal assist device. Blowing smoke into the air, he strolled out the door.

The old man gathered up the change and put it in the cash register.

It took a moment, but something clicked in Tony's head. He looked up and noticed all the others had also looked up from their cards at exactly the same time.

Then, in unison, they all looked toward the door. As they did, they could hear the bus pulling away.

THE END

Our Lady's message given through Mirjana
Dec. 2nd. 2012.

"Dear children; With motherly love and motherly patience anew I call you to live according to my Son – to spread His peace and His love – so that as my apostles you may accept God's truth with all your heart and pray for the Holy Spirit to guide you. Then you will be able to faithfully serve my Son and show His love to others with your life. According to the love of my Son and my love, as a mother, I strive to bring all of my stray children into my motherly embrace and to show them the way of faith. My children, help me in my motherly battle and pray with me that sinners may become aware of their sins and repent sincerely. Pray also for those whom my Son has chosen and consecrated in His name. Thank you."

9 781628 652307